Amateur City

A KATE DELAFIELD MYSTERY

by

Katherine V. Forrest

Spinsters I₁

2011

Copyright © 1984 by Katherine V. Forrest

Spinsters Ink
P.O. Box 242
Midway, FL 323432

Printed in the United States of America on acid-free paper

Originally published by Naiad Press 1984
Published by Alyson Press 2003
First Spinsters Ink edition 2011

Cover designer: Judy Fellows

ISBN: 978-1-935226-59-8

Other titles by Katherine V. Forrest

Apparition Alley
Liberty Square
Curious Wine
An Emergence of Green

With Special Thanks

To Montserrat Fontes, Janet Gregory, Jeffrey N. McMahan, Karen Sandler, Naomi Sloan—members of the Third Street Writers Group and fine friends, whose integrity and caring judgments have contributed to this novel and to all my work.

Chapter 1

Just before seven-thirty, Ellen O'Neil walked off the elevator into the deserted lobby of Modern Office, Incorporated. Temporarily ignoring her reason for arriving early—the mountainous filing she had sorted through yesterday—she ran a hand over coarse fabric the color of bamboo which covered the walls and elevator doors, and admired two sculptured sofas with chairs of dusky brown and salmon-pink surrounding a coffee table of stark glass and silver.

Stephie would like this, Ellen thought, gazing at vast paintings of green-toned geometric shapes, several dramatic plants with huge serrated leaves, ice-blue carpeting with wide cutouts displaying flooring of used brick. Even Stephie would think this was lovely.

As she passed Judy Markham's reception desk, huge and

black and modular and raised on a platform to majestically oversee this domain, Ellen groped in her purse for her key. She unlocked one of the double doors, went on to her office, deposited her purse and two small etchings of fishing boats she had hung in her office on her last job. Stephanie had refused to allow them on the walls of their apartment. Ellen paused. The silence was almost palpable. There was a discernible whirr, a vibration under her feet—she supposed from whatever building functions were required to maintain a livable environment on this sixteenth floor.

The filing could wait a little longer; she would use this quiet time to explore her new surroundings.

The office of her neighbor—an engineer, she remembered—contained dozens of scale model rooms enclosed in partitioned glass display cases. She crept in like a burglar and succumbed to childish pleasure in the doll's house furnishings: miniscule sofas and chairs and desks and tables, each room complete with carpeting, light fixtures, exquisitely tiny bookcases and plants.

Smiling, she walked on to the next room. Cavernous and silent, it seemed frozen in a pause between frantic bouts of activity. Desk was jammed against desk, all of them strewn and stacked with paper. In-and out-boxes spilled over their contents, the tops of filing cabinets were piled high with folders and grey metal trays heaped with paper for filing. Computer screens gaped with pale empty faces. Two microfilm units were hunched together on a drab green table pushed against a bookcase which was stuffed to untidy capacity with fat catalogues. A tiny philodendron on the perilous edge of a filing cabinet dribbled its sparse leaves not quite to the floor, the only personal touch she could find in this jumbled room with its ungenerous thin gray carpeting.

She could imagine Stephanie's opinion, hear Stephanie's voice, low and contemptuous: "A consummate example, Ellen dear, of the business world's spiritual barrenness."

She peered across the room at several shadowy cubicles flimsily partitioned off from each other, and made out faded stenciled information on a glass door: CREDIT DEPARTMENT. Luther Garrett's office. His was one of the few names she remembered from yesterday. "Luther," she had repeated after Gail Freeman. "People name their children anything." She had instantly regretted these words to her new boss whose own feminine name seemed an unfair burden for a black man to carry. But he had acknowledged her remark with a smiling nod.

She allowed the door to swing closed, and continued down the hallway, high heels sinking soundlessly into thick rust-colored carpeting. Pausing at the next door, which bore the name FRED GRAYSON on a white-lettered sign hanging from two hooks, she reflected that this was the one corner office she hadn't yet seen; Gail Freeman and Fergus Parker occupied the others—and of course Guy Adams, with his spectacular office... She smiled, remembering him.

She walked on, past other signs bearing the names HARLEY BURTON and DUANE FLETCHER, and paused before GRETCHEN PHILLIPS. She had not met these sales managers and she was curious only about Gretchen Phillips. What had it been like, her ascent to sales manager? More to the point, what kind of woman would work for a man like Fergus Parker?

She pushed open the conference room door. An imposing table, heavy, dark, glossy, was surrounded by a dozen armchairs upholstered in rich gold fabric. A painting vaguely suggestive of rolling hills and sunlight took up much of one wall. A locked glass case held an assortment of photographic equipment. She gazed for only a moment, then closed the door softly. She was near Fergus Parker's office—too near. If he by chance were in early...

Muzak swelled and waned as she strode along the carpeted hallway under the ceiling speakers, retracing her steps past Fred Grayson's office, past her own and Gail Freeman's offices, and up the hallway to the purely functional areas: supply room, photocopying, the restrooms, the kitchen and lunchroom. The aroma of coffee reached her as she came to the open doorway of the kitchen.

Who else was in early? Fergus Parker or Guy Adams, or both. It had to be, she had seen most of the other offices, and unless someone was working behind a closed door ... Most likely it was Guy Adams, she decided with a surge of pleasure. Fergus Parker wouldn't know a coffee pot from a gumball machine.

She poured coffee into a styrofoam cup, sipped appreciatively. She could at least offer Guy Adams more coffee... She picked up the coffee pot, crossed the hallway to his office.

It was empty. Sipping her coffee, she stood in the doorway looking with renewed pleasure at the furnishings in the room: the early-American ash desk with green leather inserts; an Elizabethan chair with a back of dark red wood worked into delicately carved scrolls, its seat of multi-hued blue satin; a Louis XVI armchair of ebony, with an oval back and silky peach and white upholstery; a sofa with claw-shaped legs, its fabric finely patterned silver-gray; a highly polished cherrywood table bearing a Chinese lamp the color of lime jade; a vivid red Persian rug under a coffee table of inlaid veneers; three paintings, small oils depicting scenes of the English countryside. Her eyes moved to the windows, to the distant mountains, folds of graying brown. A white mist clung to the ocean.

From down the hall came a thudding, a slight rhythmic vibration in the floor. She turned, but the corridor stretched out empty before her. Then a door slammed with an echoing violence so startling that she almost dropped the coffee pot. Automatically she took a step in the direction of Fergus Parker's office, but halted; whatever was going on down there was no affair of hers. Then there was loud and prolonged crashing and smashing of glass. It continued as she hurried along the corridor.

She slowed to a walk, glanced into Fergus Parker's office, and stood rooted. And this time she did drop the coffee pot. Fergus Parker's portable bar had fallen over, a mass of glass and spreading brown and red stain on the blond carpet. Fergus Parker sat in his big leather desk chair with arms extended in supplication, hands bloodied, eyes protruding, the pupils raisins on egg whites. A wide stream of bright blood cut a neat swath down his white shirt front from the ivory-handled implement lodged in his chest.

She began a scream, clapped both hands over her mouth. She was alone on this floor with a murderer.

Wanting to flee into an office to hide, she stood paralyzed, terrified of leaving this safely empty hallway. A murderer could be in any office she ran into. She looked around wildly. Where was the stairway? She could not remember. She stumbled on watery legs to the double doors leading to the lobby, to the elevators. She turned a knob on one of the doors, cringing at the clicking of the lock, and inched open the door. The murderer could come out to leave…

She dashed out into the lobby, took refuge behind Judy Markham's great black desk. She cowered on the floor.

EMERGENCY EXT 5000. The huge red letters on clear plastic pasted to the telephone drew her eyes. Staying low behind the desk, she slipped the telephone receiver from its hook, punched the console switch to ON, and with rigid fingers pressed the emergency digits.

"This Carlson."

"Please, I'm—"

"Can't hear you."

"Please, someone's dead—"

"Jesus! Lady, where are you?"

"Sixteen."

"Fifteen? Can't hear you."

"Sixteen." She wanted to scream, but hissed in a sibilant whisper, "Listen, there's a dead man here, I think whoever did it is still here—"

"*Jesus!* Lady, stay right where you are, don't move an *inch.*"

She hung up the receiver and hugged herself; she was cold, frozen, and she began to shudder as she sat huddled on the floor; her teeth clicked uncontrollably.

He'll hear me, she thought, he'll come out and *hear* me. I'm going to die. With Mother disappointed in me. With Stephie mad at me for being here at all.

Level with her eyes was a dial in the wall labeled MUZAK, set at four on a scale of ten. She turned it up to ten, and sat convulsed with violent shudders, the lobby reverberating to *Red*

Sails in the Sunset. An elevator light blinked on, the door opened, and two blue-clad men eased out, guns drawn.

She leaped to her feet. The guns jerked to her. "I called you! It's me!"

"*Jesus*, lady!" yelled a blond beefy guard, lowering the gun he held in two shaking hands. "You almost got yourself shot!"

"Get the lady, Rick," ordered the dark-haired guard. "I'll cover this door, you watch the door behind her."

She turned the Muzak down as the guard named Rick gingerly approached her, wide staring blue eyes fixed on the double doors behind her, his gun again raised and shaking. "You sure he's still in there?" he whispered hoarsely.

The sight of official blue uniforms and black weapons had calmed her. "I'm not sure. He might be."

"Get in the elevator, lady," the dark-haired guard called. "Now! Be quick!"

She fled across the lobby, snapping off leaves of an intervening plant in her haste. She punched LOBBY again and again. Nothing happened. She peered out to see the two guards backing toward the elevator, each with a gun trained on a set of double doors.

The dark-haired guard slid a key into a slot; the doors closed; the elevator descended. She gasped with relief and asked, "Shouldn't one of you be staying up there?"

"Not on your life," Rick said, shoving his gun deep into its holster and snapping the fastener. "Not for five-fifty an hour. Cops're on the way. What happened? What'd you see?"

"A man...stabbed..." She faltered into silence, fighting off the image.

The dark-haired guard said, "My name's Mike. That's Rick."

"Ellen," she whispered.

"Can you describe—"

"I never saw the...the killer." She closed her eyes. "I heard—"

Rick said, "You sure the guy's dead?"

"Yes," Ellen said, and burst into tears.

"Rick, lay off her. She'll have enough questions to answer."

The elevator doors opened to dozens of people milling the lobby, unable to get on an elevator. A group surged toward them.

"Out of service!" Mike shouted, inserting his key. "Elevators are out of service!"

"What the hell's going on?" demanded a portly man in a gray suit and carrying a briefcase.

"Police business. Everybody move back, please." Taking Ellen's arm, Mike led her from the elevator.

In a shrieking of sirens police cars pulled up in front, one after another, four in all, and spilled cops who ran into the building, several cradling shotguns.

"Sixteen," Mike said as five cops pushed their way through the crowd to the elevator. "Can't tell you who to look for, no description—"

"You." A mustachioed cop gestured with a shotgun at Rick. "Take us up."

"If you insist," Rick said unhappily, and inserted his key. The doors closed.

"Clear the lobby!" shouted one of the two remaining cops. They advanced on the crowd, arms extended in a shepherding motion. "Everybody back! For your own protection! Back!" In a cacaphony of sirens and thunder, another squad car and two motorcycles pulled up in front.

"Come back to the guard station with me," Mike said to Ellen. "Get you some coffee."

Stephie… I'll call Stephie… Everything will be all right .

"Please," Ellen whispered, "thanks."

Chapter 2

Detective Kate Delafield turned off Olympic Boulevard, drifted the Plymouth to a stop, and gazed down Merlin Street. It had always seemed odd to her that in this modern city she could turn off a multi-laned thoroughfare onto a side street so narrow that one car had to pull over for both to squeeze past. Like so many others, this street was crowded with tiny stucco houses of yellow and brown and white and green, and always a pink house somewhere on the block. The usual red tile roofs, the arched Spanish windows. Cracked sidewalks bordering nondescript lawns with assortments of low thick-leaved California foliage. But this street was unlike the others. This one was lined with trees. Oak. She sat looking at the black arthritic branches against the February sky, thinking achingly of Anne, missing the spreading leafy trees of their native Michigan. She reflected as she got out of her car that it was regrettable this particular murder could not have happened in May or June so that she could enjoy these trees in full bloom.

She walked around the Becker Building. Ed Taylor had preceded her by more than two hours, and an investigation team worked on the sixteenth floor; but they could all work a little longer without her. It was a savings to the taxpayers of Los Angeles if she understood the terrain; it eliminated unnecessary questions and false assumptions. Her thoroughness might arouse impatience and grumbling among the people she worked with, but the important people appreciated it. A Kate Delafield investigation was solid, meticulous, documented, a logical tapestry of fact—no sloppiness, no loose ends, no nasty surprises to ambush a district attorney, none of those holes you could drive a truck through so that a contemptuous judge would throw the case out before a jury had warmed its chairs.

The Becker Building took up half a short block, eighteen stories of small windows inset in white and gray masonry; from certain angles the structure looked pockmarked. Next door was a squat medical building, navy blue and white stucco and frame; on the other side, across Merlin Street, a sand colored building with a peeling front proclaimed from a faded sign that it was a school for computer programming.

She walked down the driveway under the Becker Building, past a banner that read MONTHLY PARKING NOW DUE. An attendant in a blue uniform shirt with stripes on the sleeves, mismatched with tan pants, ignored her. Kate walked over to a staircase, looked down and counted three levels. The staircase and the door to the lobby were the only entryways into the building from the garage. She took a notebook from her shoulder bag and pulled off the Flair pen hooked over its spine, and made brief notes.

Very tight parking, she thought. An attendant who never looks up even with squad cars parked everywhere and a murder investigation in progress. No security at all. If I had to pay for parking in the Becker Building, I'd take my chances over on Merlin Street.

She tested the door; it opened into the lobby without

necessity for a key. She exchanged nods with Hansen, who stood stolidly by the cordoned-off elevators and looked glum at the sight of her. The lobby floor was the tiny sharp mosaic tile she despised; it hurt her feet through the thin soles of her shoes.

The guard station, a low plain desk, was unattended, and she walked around behind it. There were no TV monitors, but a red receiver dangled from a hook below eye level, a red bulb above it, obviously an emergency flasher. She pulled open four drawers of the desk, one after the other. The top drawer held chocolate bars, gum, mints, lifesavers, small packets of potato chips. A sweet tooth that won't quit, or some poor bastard's trying to quit smoking, she speculated. The next drawer contained books—three Wambaugh novels and *From Here to Eternity*. In the next drawer were more pocket books, all by Harold Robbins, a half-dozen dog-eared *Hustler* magazines, a book which she picked up and dropped after a glance at its lurid cover.

"One of these guys is an eighteen-carat cretin," she muttered.

Three men in business suits came into the lobby from the garage and peered at Hansen and then fixedly at her; she ignored them. After a brief conference, Hansen allowed the men access to an elevator.

In the bottom drawer she found a ledger, and looking over several days' entries, determined that the guards checked people into the building on weekends, before 7:00 a.m. and after 7:00 p.m. on weekdays. She flipped to the day's date, February 8. Lined columns showed the date and time; visitor's signature and printed name; time of departure. Beginning at 5:45 a.m. there were twelve entries, and only one for the sixteenth floor, a florid signature. Fergus, she patiently traced with a fingernail, Parker. The signatory could not be bothered printing his name as required. Fergus Parker had come into the building at 6:53 a.m.

From the viewpoint of a guard sitting at his desk, she examined the lobby. The view of the three elevators and the only two exits from the lobby—single door to the garage, two sets of glass double doors exiting onto Olympic Boulevard—was unobstructed. Leaving the ledger on the desk, she got up and with a baleful glance at the mosaic tile, walked around the corner to the company sharing space with the lobby. Subdued gold lettering on richly gleaming walnut doors stated:

CONTEMPORARY LIFE INSURANCE, INC.
Hours Mon.—Sat. 9 a.m. — 6 p.m.

"Ralph," Kate said, coming back to the elevators, "can you give me any reason why a piece of evidence establishing the time the victim entered these premises hasn't been collected yet?" She nodded curtly toward the guard desk and the ledger.

Hansen shook his head unhappily. She stepped onto an elevator; Hansen inserted a key to release the sixteenth floor, and she rode up.

Pete Johnson was sketching the lobby on graph paper. She nodded to him, her gaze raking the lobby; uninterested in decor, she gauged the distance from the entryways to the elevators, noted the absence of a stairway. One of the double doors was propped open—not the usual procedure judging from the stapler used as a doorstop. She stepped through the doorway. A wooden sawhorse barricaded the hall to the right; she followed the murmur of male voices to her left, moved carefully around the chalk-encircled pieces of a glass coffee pot scattered across the stained carpet, and entered the corner office.

The area was being processed. The fingerprint man, his back turned, delicately brushed an edge of the ebony desk; the photographer was repacking his case. The deputy coroner talked to a bored ambulance crew, two burly black men who leaned up against the wall near their stretcher, waiting. Kate's eyes drifted over the corpse which sat with arms outstretched, the hands enclosed in paper bags tied at the wrists, an ivory-handled implement protruding from the chest. She nodded to the men in the room.

Ed Taylor, pencil poised over his notebook, completed a yawn and strolled over, skirting the smashed glass and alcohol-stained carpet. Taylor never did anything quickly. Kate watched him, disapproving of his ballooning bulk. An eighteen-year man, tall and blond, calm and humorous, he was resigned more than dedicated to his responsibilities, wanting to get the twenty years in and pull the pin. She would wager anyone that Taylor would not retire after he'd put in the twenty. Taylor would always be a cop.

"Finished," said the photographer.

She said, "You get plenty of angles of all this glass?"

The photographer did not turn around. "Everything. Dammit, check my log. I got everything."

The ambulance crew moved to the body. Kate looked at the deputy coroner.

"He's been stabbed," Everson said.

The men chuckled, and Kate smiled. The ambulance crew, ready to hoist the corpse onto the stretcher, paused to guffaw.

"Time of death between seven-thirty and eight," Everson said, grinning.

Kate said, "Blood on the killer?"

"Possible. Could very well be. Bleeding was localized but there's a stain on the desk—on impact, from the directionality. A spurt got the killer's hand or sleeve at the very least."

"Victim sitting like that when he got it?"

Everson hesitated, fingering a pencil-thin moustache. "It's odd, Kate. A hundred and eighty degree wound." He flicked a well-manicured hand at the corpse, and she walked over to have a closer look. "Usually there's a downward angle to a knife thrust but this one's almost level. He might've been standing, leaned back from the blow, fell back into the chair. Or sitting, in the process of getting up. The weapon's a beaut, isn't it?" She was bent down, examining the curved, intricate ivory handle. "Too faceted to pick up a print."

"The office manager ID'd the body," Taylor said. "Says it's the victim's letter opener. Wide blade, edges like a razor, he says."

Kate stepped back, and the black men hoisted the body. Everson continued, "A weapon like that, a two-year old could've done it. Went through that whale blubber like butter."

"Fat fucking son of a bitch," one of the black men grunted as they wrapped and secured the hulk on the stretcher.

Again, Kate surveyed the desk, the shattered glass. "That kind of wound, Walt, any possibility of suicide?"

"Kate," Taylor said, "a witness heard somebody—"

"Walt?" Kate interrupted, ignoring Taylor.

Again Everson hesitated. "Could explain the level entry of the weapon, and no defensive cuts on him, either. But there're no experimental wounds, no visible sign of other pricking of the skin. The shirt's nice and neat, no cuts anywhere from hesitation marks. And you know how they hesitate, Kate. How often they take clothing off, or at least push it aside. No evidence of cadaveric spasm—no death grip of the weapon, no immediate rigor like there sometimes is with suicide." Everson glanced at his chain-bracelet watch. "Three hours now and no sign of it yet."

"But still, is it possible?"

"Possible. We'll both need a much closer look."

"Sure." She turned to Taylor. "Ed, how many people in this office?"

Taylor consulted his notes. "Forty-one."

"That's a lot of interviews, Walt."

"And if it's homicide," Taylor said, "we got a lot of people we can't segregate and not much time before they ignore instructions and start gabbing to each other."

"Meaning you want an immediate autopsy." Everson pursed his lips, stroked his moustache again, glanced at the stretcher. "This one looks clean and tidy enough. And it's Tuesday, it's always slow on Tuesdays. Call you as soon as we set it up."

The group soon left, talking and chuckling among themselves as they followed the ambulance crew and stretcher.

Taylor turned back pages of his notes, and Kate settled a hip on the edge of the teak credenza and took out her notebook. She asked, not looking up, "You heard?"

"Yeah. I figured they'd plea bargain down to second, but involuntary manslaughter—Jesus Christ, God damn it, Kate—"

She tuned him out, taking in details of the room again as he continued his diatribe on the insanities of the court system. She had been in court this morning, expecting to testify. The case had been continued to May. The victim had been only seventeen, her killer twenty-two and with a rap sheet as long as her arm; he'd been in trouble since Kate's days in Juvenile. He was typical of today's criminal—and that was what disturbed her, more than the plea bargain. Younger—they were younger, with drugs in their past and present, and they were casual about their crimes, committing without thought acts of utter savagery. And while female crime was also increasing, she had read projections that soon one out of three American men would have in his past a perpetration of violence…. The thin blue line of men and women who did their best to protect and to serve—how much longer could they hold back such ferocity? Well, she did her job, it was all she could do. "Ed," she finally said, her tone harsh, "it's history."

He sighed, looked at his notes. "This one's not suicide, Kate. Doesn't feel right. And that corpse looked as surprised as hell."

"True," she conceded. "What've you got so far?"

"Code three all units at seven-forty-two." Taylor read dispassionately from the crime report and his notes. "A one-eighty-seven, suspect on premises. Premises secured approximately eight a.m. We have a complete list of everyone on the upper floors of the building after it was sealed—"

Kate interjected acidly, "For all the good that'll do."

Taylor glanced up only briefly and then continued, "Ellen Rose O'Neil arrived approximately seven-twenty a.m., heard noise, found the victim approximately seven-forty. Did not observe the killer …"

Taylor's notes were always factual if not comprehensive, and she listened with concentration. Overall examination of the scene was virtually complete: photographs, sketches, measurements, descriptions, fingerprinting. The necessity for elimination fingerprints had been explained to the employees; all had expressed cooperation. Kate jotted one-and two-word notes.

"Hair tidy, body slightly turned but trunk position normal," Taylor droned. "Eyes open. Diamond ring, Cartier wrist watch, three hundred cash in the desk drawer. No signs of disorder except for blood smears on the desk, victim's fingers sliding off. Blood marks on the liquor cart, victim's left hand, it looks like."

Kate walked around behind the desk, gauging the distance and angles between the desk, chair, spilled cart.

Taylor consulted a sketch spread across the seat of a chair in front of the desk. "The cart was pushed from its usual position of nine feet eight inches to a proximity of twenty-six inches from the body, according to the tracks."

Kate knelt next to the overturned cart which was covered with fingerprint powder, lifted a corner with her pen, glanced at the glossy dried reddish-brown stains.

"Blood marks are along the railing," Taylor said unnecessarily. "Indicating the victim grabbed it, pulled it over."

She nodded and moved on her knees, scrutinizing the wheel marks in the carpet. She sank her pen into a set of deep grooves. "Cart usually sits right here. When was it moved? Why? Why would it be so close to his desk at seven o'clock in the morning? Let's check with the cleaning people to see where it was last night."

Taylor made a note.

She got to her feet, brushed at the knees of her gray pants. "Lots of prints on the cart."

Taylor shrugged. "Dozens."

"Desk contents?"

"All itemized, nothing unusual except for the cash. Ditto the credenza. Nothing's missing from the office, according to the office manager. But then he's black—"

"Anything else?" she said curtly. Taylor's racial prejudice, which surfaced at any opportunity, continually irked her.

Taylor flipped note pages. "Cigar butt and ash. Appears to be the victim's but we collected it."

She nodded, her glance again traversing the room: the cream-colored leather sofa and armchair, the glass table topped by an abstract silver sculpture, the bookcase containing a clutter of plaques and trophies. Her gaze lingered on the fouled blond carpet; the darkening bloodstain outlined in chalk on the ebony desk dirty with fingerprint powder and barren except for two Cross pens imbedded in a marble base; the immense leather chair forever divested of its daily occupant. She strolled over and examined three black-framed, autographed photographs on the wall—Fergus Parker shaking hands with Lyndon Johnson, Barry Goldwater, Richard Nixon. She moved to the family photograph on the bookcase. "Notification?"

"Wife. His third marriage. A boy eleven, girl thirteen, in schools back East. The office manager drove out there. Santa Monica. Insisted on going. Hansen took him. The wife is nicely alibied. From six-thirty to eight she was at the next door neighbor's. And I'd say she didn't use a pro."

Kate nodded. "I'd say not. He'd use his own weapon. And make the hit on familiar, predictable territory." She continued to study the photograph of Fergus Parker's family.

Taylor said, "Spend a lot of time with bibs tucked under their chins, don't they? All three porkers, like him."

You should talk, Kate thought. "What about the O'Neil woman?"

"Nice lady. Thirty-one. Cool. Attractive, smart. Handles herself very calm and determined."

Delicately, Taylor cleared his throat. Alerted, Kate glanced at him; but his gaze was fixed on the Santa Monica mountains, clear and vivid in the distance. "A roommate came. Girl friend."

Gay, she thought. Or at least he thinks so.

"Spent half an hour with her, wanted her to go home, *insisted*. Left mad as hell." He glanced at her. "She's a prof at UCLA. Economics."

So they may be gay, Kate thought in amusement, but apparently not card-carrying dykes. She said bluntly, "The O'Neil woman, she a possible?"

Taylor's grin was swift, ingratiating. "She'd have to get a mad on awful quick. She's new, second day here. Unless it's her period." He grinned again, then shrugged as Kate did not smile. "We're gonna have a good time with this one, Kate. This Fergus Parker's popular as Hitler. These people here, when they heard, I thought they were gonna join hands and sing ding dong the witch is dead. The only one who looked sorry was his secretary—" Taylor looked through his notes. "—Billie Sullivan. Weird. Walks like she's got her body on backwards."

Kate chuckled. "It *is* a little different, Ed. A pillar of the community instead of the usual, like MacKenzie on Friday."

Taylor pushed out his fleshy lips. "Mrs. MacKenzie calls nine times a day. Husband gets bashed with a tire iron in the May Company parking lot, no witnesses, she can't understand why we haven't made a collar yet. One of these people you talk to, you're on Wilshire, she's on Sunset. I explain the May Company parking lot was not exactly loaded with clues, she keeps saying she's a taxpayer."

Kate said impatiently, "Don't waste any more time with her, have her talk to Lieutenant Bell. What's the situation with the employees here?"

"They're plenty nervous. Working, more or less." Taylor ran a hand through lank blond hair, pausing a moment to scratch. "The black office manager, he seems sharp enough. He got 'em all calmed down. Hansen took the O'Neil woman's statement, I talked to her, we took her in but she didn't give us much—"

"Wait a minute," Kate said. "Go back in your notes about her. About finding the victim."

Taylor turned over two pages in his notebook. "She was in the kitchen getting coffee. Stepped out into the north hallway, walked up to the west hallway carrying the coffee pot to offer some to Guy Adams who she thought was in. Heard running steps, a door slam, the sound coming from the southwest end of the corridor, then crashing glass. Ran down the hallway, saw the victim and dropped the coffee pot—"

"Okay," Kate said. "You said she was in the kitchen getting coffee. Who made the coffee?"

"Why she, uh, I assu—" Taylor caught himself. "I don't have a note on that, Kate."

"I want the coffee pot. And the glass in here. I want the coffee pot dusted. I assume," she said, placing sarcastic emphasis on the word as Taylor busily wrote, "no one went through the other office waste baskets for paper cups, checked desks for warm coffee?"

Taylor shifted his feet. "The wastebasket in here was clean. The executive washroom, no signs of blood but we chemical tested, we collected some used paper towels—"

"Maybe the victim's," Kate said shortly.

"Yeah, right." Taylor's broad face was slightly flushed. "Myself, I saw a coffee mug on the kitchen counter, fancy hunting scene on it. Empty. We can still bag all the other trash, Kate."

Kate thought: I suppose *I am* a bitch to work with, but people can be so *damn* stupid. "Think about it, Ed," she said coldly, "what earthly good would that do now?" She asked after a deepening silence, "Press been and gone?"

Taylor's voice was stiff. "Kovich handled it."

"Ed, remember the one three months ago, the guy who shot his way out of the Bank of America?"

"Yeah, oh God yeah, crazy Garcia." Taylor's hostility softened as he remembered. "God, the mess. God, the witnesses." His blue eyes rolled up in mournful memory. "God, the paperwork."

"There's a lot of people here too, Ed. We need to find a handle fast, a pattern, a direction to go."

Taylor nodded. "The office manager's set us up in the conference room. You pull down the shades, it's a fancy interrogation room."

"Suggestions?" She was being only partly conciliatory; she was team supervisor, and she had worked with Taylor—who had reached Detective-one nine years ago and had remained there—on too many investigation teams.

"You'll want to talk to Ellen O'Neil and the office manager. This one shouldn't take long, Kate. Whoever did it knew this guy—it figures. And that means we're in Amateur City. And that means we'll get him. So we split up, move fast. You take the managers, they're more your style. I'll take the service people. Anybody that looks like a half-way possible we take down for interrogation."

"Good." She was pleased. "I'll talk to the black office manager first. He have a name?"

"Girl's name," Taylor temporized, flipping pages. "Gail. Freeman. Right now he's in the conference room with the other managers. Figuring a way to handle things till their home office names a new head honcho."

Kate accompanied Taylor down the hall to the door marked CONFERENCE ROOM. Through the door could be heard, faintly, laughter. She said wryly, "They're not exactly holding a wake for Mr. Fergus Parker."

She rapped, opened the door. A woman, and five men, one

of them black, stared at her with rapidly sobering faces. Taylor said easily, "This is my partner, Detective Delafield. She'll be coordinating our investigation."

Well aware of the psychological value of her badge, especially in a group, Kate extracted the leather case from her shoulder bag and flipped it open to display her shield and ID card.

"Gail Freeman." The black man had immediately stood, and he leaned over the wide glossy table to shake hands.

Swiftly, she evaluated him: Light-skinned, no more than five-eight, maybe one-thirty-five. Late thirties, early forties—possibly older. Erect posture, dapper. Simple dark suit, crisp beige shirt, subdued tie. Cropped, well-barbered hair. Buffed nails, firm handshake.

He had begun introductions, and she turned her attention to the group around the conference table.

Fred Grayson, wearing a green striped shirt and green tie, adjusted horn-rimmed glasses over owlish hazel eyes as he rose to shake hands. He nodded, his head a mass of regular waves of thick gray-brown hair.

Harley Burton, pristine white shirtsleeves rolled up over thick arms knotted with muscles, seized her hand and pumped it vigorously; as he sat down he yanked on a black and white patterned tie, and stared at her with piercing dark eyes.

Duane Fletcher ran a tidying hand over the dark fringe circling his perfectly spherical bald head, and shook hands with a moist hand. His smile was shy. He wore a bright yellow shirt with a tie of yellow and purple stripes.

Gretchen Phillips, dark-haired, tiny, very pretty in a filmy lilac blouse, nodded and smiled, her delicate lips accented by pale lipstick; she looked at Kate with cool blue-gray eyes alert with appraisal and curiosity.

Guy Adams' handshake was warm and firm, and several seconds longer than necessary. His jacket and tie were the color of rich cream, his shirt the color of coffee. She took in the reddish-blond hair carefully styled to compensate for its thinness, the green eyes not quite focused on her. Turned out like a Brooks Brothers ad, she thought, unsuccessfully resisting the impulse of dislike.

She said, "I trust all of you understand the importance of giving any information you have to us, not discussing it with each other until our interviews are complete. Any of you may possess information of a value—"

There was a sharp rap, and the door swung open. In increasing amazement Kate stared at the young woman who sidled into the room. A tight fuzzy aqua sweater covered thin slouched shoulders and almost imperceptible breasts; bare bony knees poked out from below a wrinkled khaki skirt that outlined stick-like thighs receding toward a pelvis and stomach which were thrust forward. A pointed chin jutted aggressively. The woman held a stack of folders carelessly under one arm; smoke drifted upward from a cigarette cupped in the palm of the other hand.

"Detective Delafield, this is Billie Sullivan," Gail Freeman said in a flat tone. "Fergus Parker's secretary."

"A lady dick," Billie Sullivan rasped, extending a hand. "The boss would be pissed as hell."

Kate managed to smother a laugh, but not her smile. She grasped skeletal fingers that felt like a collection of dry twigs. From around the conference table there were coughs and cleared throats; Gretchen Phillips chuckled softly.

Billie Sullivan said, "So how do you like the Modern Office way of terminating employees?" Her laugh was like the snapping and breaking of glass.

Gretchen Phillips chuckled again. Gail Freeman said sternly, "Billie, did you finish that special report for Philadelphia?"

"About. I gave the shit part to Ellie." She added, "The office idiot, likes to type numbers." This last remark seemed directed at Kate, but Billie Sullivan's wide-set greenish eyes looked off each in a different direction, and Kate was not quite certain. Billie Sullivan pushed wispy carroty hair off a pale freckled forehead, and dragged at her cigarette, cheeks sinking inward with the suction; she hissed out smoke in a thin jet stream.

"Billie, watch that ash on this light carpet," Fred Grayson warned.

Casting a glance of undisguised contempt at Fred Grayson, she deposited the folders in an untidy heap on the conference room table and flicked inch-long ash into a palm without flinching; then she moved in two long loping strides, cadaverous body slouched into the shape of a question mark, and released the ash from her palm into a wastebasket. She lifted a thick sandal and stubbed out her cigarette against the serrated sole, sending sparks cascading. She dropped in the blackened butt.

"For chrissake," muttered Fred Grayson.

"Thank you, Billie." Gail Freeman's voice was distant and formal. "Please bring me that report the moment it's finished."

"Certainly. Sir," she added, and grinned, revealing wolfish yellow teeth. A blue eyelid drooped over an unfocused eye. For whom the wink was intended, Kate could not guess. Billie Sullivan loped to the door, and turned. "Pleasure meeting you, lady copper." The door swung shut on a sound that was again like shattering glass—Billie Sullivan's laughter.

"Gail," Fred Grayson, said, "that—that woman—"

"One of the first items on the new agenda," Gail Freeman said curtly. He rose. "Why don't we continue this meeting in your office, Fred? I've promised use of this room to the detectives."

Guy Adams immediately got to his feet; Gretchen Phillips gathered up the folders on the table. "Mr. Freeman," Kate said, "would you please remain."

The managers trooped out, Duane Fletcher casting a nervous glance over his shoulder at Gail Freeman, as if at a victim facing an uncertain but surely grim fate.

Kate said quietly, "An ugly business, Mr. Freeman."

"Gail." Freeman crossed his arms and looked directly at her. "Worst thing I ever saw was a guy that rolled into my foxhole without a head and his guts falling out."

Kate said softly, "I was in Da Nang. Marine Supply Corps. But I didn't see things like that till I joined LAPD."

"Pusan," Freeman said, and grinned at her puzzlement. "Different war. Korea. I'm older than I look."

"Fifty-three, Kate," Taylor said.

Taylor was already wasting time, she thought with irritation. "Mr. Freeman, would it be possible to make another room available to us in addition to this one?"

"Luther Garrett left for San Francisco yesterday. His office is in the service bay."

"I'll take that one, Kate," Taylor said. "Be in there interviewing the service people if you need me."

"We have a paging system," Freeman said.

"Good." She nodded dismissal at Taylor. "Mr. Freeman, I understand the victim was VP of operations. Who's in charge now?"

"No one, officially. That decision'll have to come out of Philadelphia, the home office. May take several days."

"Understandable. But didn't Fergus Parker delegate when he was gone or on vacation?"

Freeman shook his head. "You could always get him by phone. But if he decided it wasn't urgent, he'd have your ass hanging from a flagpole."

Kate grinned. "I worked for somebody like that years ago. We called him Insecure Sam."

"I'd never call Fergus Parker insecure," Freeman said drily. "Paranoid, maybe."

"Sounds like you didn't care much for him," she said casually, watching him.

Freeman looked at her steadily. "Let me put it this way. I made the identification of the body. I thought the knife looked well in him."

Kate cleared her throat vigorously to avoid laughing.

"You must not be too concerned about being a suspect."

Freeman's laugh was short. "I'll just be one on a list."

"Really?" She tucked her notebook into her bag to encourage response. "Who else would like to see Fergus Parker dead?"

Freeman shook his head, and leaned against the table, hands in his pockets. "I speak only for Gail Freeman. Especially under the circumstances. I listen to gossip, I don't spread it."

She studied his austere face, the caramel flesh drawn across ascetic bones. Even with his jacket unbuttoned and tie slightly askew, he managed a tidy elegance. She said coolly, "Don't you want to see a killer caught?"

Freeman shrugged. "All I am is curious. Who it was that popped his cork."

"Not necessarily he. A woman just as easily."

"Yes. Forgive my prejudiced and sexist remark."

Kate was amused, but she said sternly, "Mr. Freeman, I expect you to be cooperative, within reason."

"I will be, within reason." There was not the slightest hint of sarcasm in his tone.

"Do you know of any reason why the dead man would want to harm himself?"

"Harm himself? You mean…*suicide?*" Gail Freeman chuckled; his chuckle became a laugh, gaining rapidly in volume and resonance and infectiousness.

Kate found herself grinning. "I take it the answer is no."

"Most emphatically no. The man was lord of his universe. Loved using and abusing his power. Somebody did it to him and you can take that to the bank."

Kate said, "Would you mind taking me around the office so I can get a better feel for the layout? To the lobby first, I think."

"Sure." He opened the door for Kate, walked with her down the corridor. "One question. Do you have any objection if I fire Billie Sullivan?"

"Why now? Wouldn't you want her for continuity's sake, when the new man comes in?"

"She wouldn't contribute anything useful, just spread poison." Freeman's voice rose in forcefulness. "She does no work to speak of. And creates personnel problems. The little work Parker gave her she always farmed out to the other women. If I ever challenged her, Parker always said she was too busy. The other employees despise her."

"I can well understand," Kate said. "My—I had a friend in an office politics situation like that. Ended up quitting. But I ask you to hold up just a little longer. Over the span of the initial investigation. Because of her position in relation to the victim. She may have useful information you're not aware of."

"Your objections are well within reason." Freeman nodded toward the hallway. "Can I have that office cleaned up? Smells like a sewer with all that spilled booze."

"Afraid not. The crime scene will have to be sealed pending

review of our reports, till we notify you. We'll close and seal the door, release the hallway as soon as our team finishes. All those bottles in there, I assume Fergus Parker was a drinking man?"

"Not to my knowledge. At least not during working hours. We kept ice for him in the kitchen refrigerator but he used it only for visitors."

Kate took out her notebook and roughly sketched the main features of the lobby: the elevators, the doors, the receptionist's desk. Gail Freeman said conversationally, "Being a female detective must present its challenges."

She felt the familiar heavy weariness at being reminded of her singularity. The tired knowledge that always she was silhouetted against her background. Always.

Always. Growing up, she had been taller and stronger, more aggressive than the other girls; in look and manner, hopelessly unfeminine by their standards. Among similarly uniformed women in the Marine Corps, she had been resented for her unusual physical strengths and command presence. She had been the woman reluctantly singled out in her division of the Los Angeles Police Department for one advancement after another as LAPD, in stubborn fighting retreat, gradually succumbed to increasing pressures for change.

And always there had been that one most essential difference: she was a woman who desired only other women.

That she had always stood out in her differentness had no longer mattered after Anne. As long as there had been Anne to love her for all of her differentness...

She looked at Gail Freeman. Had she welcomed a discussion of this topic, there was no time, and with Gail Freeman currently a suspect, it was hardly appropriate. She said, gauging the distance in both her voice and her face, "Being a black manager must present its challenges."

Freeman did not reply. He leaned against the reception desk, arms crossed, watching her.

This man is a very class act, she decided. She said, "The receptionist, would you ask her to come out here?"

"Sure. Judy's filing in the service bay." He picked up the receiver on the console behind the black desk, punched a number; his amplified voice came out of the loudspeaker in the ceiling interrupting the Muzak: "Judy Markham, please come to the lobby."

Scant moments later, a blue-eyed, large-breasted young woman Kate judged to be in her early twenties came into the lobby, tucking the tail of a white silken blouse into a red plaid skirt, flinging long straight blonde hair off her face with a practiced toss of her head. Kate looked at her with pleasure.

"Judy Markham, this is Detective Delafield."

Judy Markham looked at her in consternation. "Jeez, this mean I can't come back on the desk yet? Filing's the *pits*."

Some people, Kate thought sadly, should never be allowed to open their mouths. But she smiled and said gently, "I think everyone feels that way about filing. I'd like you to explain some things about your job. Would you answer a few questions?"

"Sure. I heard we had a lady cop here, it's great. Uh, what do I call you?" She looked Kate over doubtfully.

"Detective," supplied Gail Freeman.

"Oh." She brightened, then shrieked, "Like *Cagney and Lacey!*"

"Somewhat," Kate said, gritting her teeth.

"Judy," Gail Freeman said, grinning, "stop wasting the detective's time. Just answer her questions."

Kate learned that Judy Markham first recorded, then announced all visitors; that she controlled entry through the doors on either end of the lobby by dialing a two-digit code on her console to release the electronic locks, which relocked after a thirty-second delay. And that employees had their own key for after hours, but she customarily dialed them in during the day.

"So no one can get in before or after hours unless they have a key," Kate said.

"Nope."

"What about ex-employees?"

"I collect their keys as a matter of routine," Freeman said. "For security."

Kate smiled. "Ever change the locks?"

Freeman shook his head, his chuckle rueful. "I hear you."

Kate examined the visitor's log. "Miss Markham, anybody unusual visit Mr. Parker recently?"

Judy Markham flicked a glance at Gail Freeman. "Whaddya mean, recently?"

"The past few weeks or so. Mr. Freeman," Kate said casually, "why don't I call you in a few minutes when I'm through out here?"

"Sure." Hands in his pockets, Gail Freeman strolled off and let himself out of the far end of the lobby with his key.

Judy Markham jabbed at a name in the book. "*This* creep. This bald sweaty little *shit!* Did he come on to me? I like told him *four times* I gotta *boyfriend.* He said El Grosso in there—" She gestured violently at Fergus Parker's office, "—said I gave him *head jobs!* All the *time!* He offered me *fifty bucks!* I hope El Grosso took six *hours* to die!"

Kate said soberly, impressed by her fury, "Did Mr. Parker ever come on to you?"

"With his big fat fucking mouth," she spat. "Remarks, you know? Couldn't say hello, he'd say something about my tits. 'Good morning, Mr. Parker,' she mimicked. " 'Good morning, Judy, nice sweater, color makes you look tasty as ice cream, yum yum.' *Ychhh!* And look at me? Like he's *fucking* me with those piggy popeyes!"

Will I ever get used to how easily the young women use the language, Kate thought. "You didn't want to tell me this in front of Mr. Freeman. Why not?"

"He'd of got upset. He's a good guy."

"Miss Markahm, it's his *job* to get upset. Why didn't you complain to him?"

"What was I s'poseta complain about?"

"Harassment. There are increasingly stringent penalties in this state against sexual harassment."

She laughed, mocking peals. "Come on, Cagney. You know how it is. I'm a blonde, a receptionist. I'd be up shit's creek, I ever complain. Laws don't make anything any different. You think I take shit? I gotta good friend, Susie's a stewardess. Cabin attendants they call 'em now. You oughtta hear Susie. Guys figure they got a license. Not all of 'em like El Grosso but I get remarks all the time. And anyway, you think any place's any different from this? You really think that?"

"I really don't know, Miss Markham," Kate said softly. "I only know laws are meant to protect people."

"Hey, Cagney, you're nice." Judy Markham tossed the hair back from her face again, ingenuous blue eyes focused ambiguously on Kate's. "You can call me Judy."

She kept her face expressionless, her voice carefully toneless. "I appreciate that, Miss Markham. Would you page Mr. Freeman?"

"Ah shit. You gonna make me go back and file?"

"Just a little longer. Until we can release the floor for public entry. I'll appreciate your patience."

"Sure, Cagney." Again the ambiguous gaze. Judy Markham sauntered from the lobby, hips swaying.

Sketching in her notebook with intense concentration, ignoring curious faces peering at her, Kate silently walked the hallways, recording names, pacing distances to the staircase, the lobby. Gail Freeman strolled beside her, hands in his pockets, laconically giving names and titles. Again they walked past the crime scene; past Billie Sullivan who sat at her desk running raw-boned fingers through strings of carroty hair as she spoke on the phone; past a door marked MEN PRIVATE.

"The executive washroom," Gail Freeman said. "Opens with a key, of course. Quite a flap when Gretchen Phillips was promoted to sales manager but excluded from the washroom. She didn't care a fig but the rest of the women were mad as hornets." He chuckled reminiscently.

"What did you do?"

"Nothing. I only do something about what I can do something about." He paused before the next door. "Like here. This is word processing. Quite an operation." He pushed open the heavy door.

An incessant rat-a-tat echoed from the machines operated by a row of women attached to earphones. White print blipped frantically down a half dozen luminous green computer screens. One of the operators, a tiny black woman, left her computer to rush to a giant orange trash can, dump an armload of paper, rush back to her console. Two telexes chugged out yellow paper. An Oriental woman gesticulated in eloquent frustration as she spoke on the phone. A telefax whirred rhythmically.

Kate gazed at the maelstrom of activity, noting the relatively low noise level. The ceiling and walls were of sound-absorbent porous cork; the brown carpet, unsightly with excisions—apparently for the movement of electrical outlets—was unusually thick. Four or five women had looked up as the door opened; they waved to Gail Freeman, who acknowledged them with a smile and an upraised hand. He let the door swing shut; the sound cut off abruptly.

"A factory," Kate said.

"Yes. And that group in there, they're such good people, they work so hard ... Ever been in a factory?"

"No." She walked slowly on down the hall with him.

"I come from a blue-collar town. Toledo. Worked in a wheel factory. The noise—enough to explode your brains. That's how that room used to be, till I managed to get the composition walls, the carpet. But without Guy's help I could never have made those changes."

"Why not, Mr. Freeman?"

"Budget." He said the word the way she had heard other people utter the word fuck. "Fergus Parker told me there was no room in the budget. But even in this uncertain economy, sales down, earnings down, Fergus Parker thought nothing of taking the entire sales staff to San Francisco for a quote business meeting unquote, thousands of dollars, all expenses paid, nothing's too good. And I've been to those quote meetings unquote and know how little quote business unquote is done. But he couldn't find any room in his budget for a few thousand bucks to make that room liveable. Guy Adams was the one who told me to do it, just give him the bills and he'd have the company take care of it."

"How does Mr. Adams have that authority?"

"Had that authority," Gail Freeman corrected sadly. "He's a nephew of the owner—but old Guy Adams died last year and the company's been reorganizing ever since." He paused in the hallway. "This is Guy's office. It's quite an office."

Kate did not look at the office, but at the man sitting on the corner of his desk talking on the phone, facing the windows, his back to them. Again fighting the impulse of dislike, she studied the carefully combed reddish-blond hair, the elegant breadth of the shoulders, the tapered slenderness of the body, the trim waist and hips emphasized by the perfectly cut cream-colored jacket. "I'll take care of it, consider it done," Guy Adams was saying, his voice soft and husky, reminiscent of an actor's voice she had heard in an old war movie during the late hours of the last sleepless night. Aldo Ray, she remembered with satisfaction. Then Guy Adams hung up and turned around and looked at her with startled, widening eyes. She inventoried his features: thin straight nose, a wide mouth with finely shaped lips, a thin face of fine bones. The features of an aristocrat. She nodded to Guy Adams and walked on.

She went into the kitchen, studied its layout, then continued down the hall. She paused outside the closed door of Gail Freeman's corner office. "Do all the managers close their doors when they're away from the office?"

"Only when they leave for the night, usually. I always close mine if I leave during the day because I have personnel information in my office. The other managers will too if they've been working on something confidential."

"Like what?"

"Oh, salary projections, for instance. I don't believe many of them actually lock their doors at night. I'm always reminding Guy to close and lock his, I chewed him out again just yesterday. It's the only one with anything of real value. But the elevators and staircase are secured at night, the cleaning people are very reliable, we've had no instances at all of theft."

"I see. What—" She broke off. In the office next to Gail Freeman's she saw a woman with shoulder-length wavy brown hair, her chair swiveled so that her gaze was apparently fixed on the gray towers of downtown Los Angeles. Kate took Gail Freeman's arm, led him down the hall a few steps. "Who is that?"

"Ellen O'Neil, my new assistant. She found the—well, you know that, of course. She's very upset, as you can imagine."

"Yes. Detective Taylor mentioned that you informed Mrs.

Parker. How did she take the news?"

Freeman cleared his throat. "Well, she was shocked, of course." He gave Kate a gauging look, then said, "She told me first thing she'd do would be to call her kids back East, have them come home. Then she told me she had lots of black, it was the color she mostly wore once she married Fergus Parker. Then she poured herself a highball glass full of scotch, no water, no ice. Then the grieving widow asked how much insurance I thought Fergus Parker might have."

Kate was unable to smother a smile. "How much does he have?"

"The home office'll call her with the exact figure. But at his salary I'd say at least a quarter million automatically, more if he picked up any of the electives. The widow Parker should be pretty comfortable. Might even buy herself a red dress."

"Indeed. Mr. Freeman, I'd like you to supply a complete list of current employees and their addresses, and all transferred and ex-employees over the period of time the victim has worked in this office."

"We can punch that out of the computer with no problem."

"Are the employment records on file in this office, or Philadelphia?"

"Here."

"We'll have to have those files pulled for our inspection."

Freeman frowned slightly. "I believe I'd better run that one past the legal people in Philly."

"Whatever. I imagine a simple search warrant will be sufficient to satisfy them. Are you filling the breach for Mr. Parker? Since he doesn't have a designated successor?"

"We've decided that two of us should. Myself and Fred Grayson."

Kate consulted her sketch. "Sales manager, southeast corner office."

"That's the one. Senior manager in service time. Anything you need in terms of office functions or personnel, that's my bailiwick normally."

"Good. I'd like to see Miss O'Neil now. Would you have her come to the conference room?"

Fergus Parker | Billie Sullivan | Exec Rest Room | Computer, Word Proccesing & Telex | Guy Adams

Double Doors

Stair-way

Conference Room

Judy Markham

Kitchen & Lunch Room

Gretchen Phillips

Xerox & Mail Room

Duane Fletcher

Supplies

Harley Burton

Stair-way

Double Doors

Rest Room

Fred Grayson

Customer Service & Credit

Luther Garrett

Matt Bradford | Ellen O'Neill | Gail Freeman

Chapter 3

As she walked toward the conference room, Ellen thought warmly of Guy Adams, the single person in this company other than Gail Freeman—who was, after all, her boss—to seek her out and express concern and sympathy. This man who had been so charmingly at ease yesterday—with whom she had discovered, through several elegantly bound volumes she had noticed in his bookcase, a mutual love for the English poets— had been today scarcely able to speak and had looked ill, she thought, the gentle green eyes stricken and dull. But then he was obviously the kind of man who would be more upset than most by what had happened.

As she reached the door of the conference room she felt a pull of curiosity about the detective waiting for her, and smiled again at Gail Freeman's sardonic description: "Kojak's a lovable marshmallow compared to this lady. Warmest thing about her is her corduroy jacket."

Ellen opened the door. "Detective Delafield," she said.

The woman sitting across from her at the conference table, her dark hair salted with gray, her corduroy jacket a light soft green, was examining a sketch, holding a leather-bound notebook sideways in strong square hands. She looked at Ellen with light blue eyes that were cool, level, and candid.

Ellen stared at her. *Stephie can talk all she wants about not being able to tell for sure, but if this woman's not a lesbian then neither am I.*

At the sight of Ellen O'Neil, Kate felt a twisting sensation, an excruciating pleasure-pain that became mostly pain. The same height—give or take half an inch. Hips only a little thinner, well-shaped breasts like Anne's, the contours outlined by the soft beige blouse. Lips a little fuller, nose straighter. Prettier. But then Anne had looked like no one else with those features that all tilted upward—delicate bow lips and eyes darker than Ellen O'Neil's—slanty like a Chinaman's, Anne had always said…Anne's hair lighter and not so neat as Ellen O'Neil's, with those unruly curls clustered at the nape of her neck …

Ellen was startled, puzzled; the detective had looked up from her notebook, her eyes swiftly traveling up Ellen's body to focus on her face, the light blue eyes narrowing in what appeared to be pain.

"Detective Delafield," she said again.

Not much different from Anne's voice, that low throatiness of Anne's…

"Detective Delafield?" Ellen looked at her intently, in concern.

Kate cleared her throat. "Excuse me, you reminded… I was thinking about something else."

"With great concentration." Ellen smiled, to coax softness into that strong face, those grim features.

Oh God, it's so unfair…her smile is like Anne's. She smoothed a fresh page in her notebook and cleared her throat again. "Sit down please, Miss O'Neil. I know this has been hard for you, I know you've told your story several times already, had it recorded. But I'd like you to go over it again. Very slowly. Include every detail you can think of. Starting with where and when you parked your car."

Ellen relaxed. She had always been comfortable around people—especially women—like Stephie, like Kate Delafield, with authority in their voices, strength in their faces, deliberation in their gestures and manner. "Well, I parked in the garage at twenty after seven—"

"How did you know the time?"

She spoke glibly, having already answered this question twice, "I was listening to the news on KFWB. They announce the time constantly in the morning. And I was annoyed I hadn't figured the time better, I could've slept a little longer. This is my first job in more than a year. I'm not used to getting up this early." She thought, if she pursues this she'll find out I live with a woman...

But Kate Delafield said, "I see. Was there anyone in the garage or lobby that you recognized?"

"No, but I'm new. I know hardly anyone."

"What about the people that you do know? Did you see any of them?"

"No."

"Who would you recognize? Name them."

In expanding warmth and pride, she was absorbing the knowledge that this impressive and highly professional woman was the detective in charge of this murder investigation—and a lesbian. "Well, Gail of course. And Guy. Guy Adams. I'm not used to calling managers by first name but that's the custom here—" She broke off her attempt at conversation as she met the cool blue glance, and continued hurriedly, "I was introduced to Luther Garrett yesterday. Some people from the service bay and word processing. I don't know their names but I'd know their faces. Billie Sullivan. That's all."

"Are you sure?"

After a moment's pause, she nodded.

"Positive?"

"Positive." She was annoyed.

"What about Judy Markham?"

"Oh. Yes. I forgot about her."

Knowing Kate Delafield's silence was deliberate, Ellen felt heat rise to her face.

Kate watched her; her face had a slight ruddiness like Anne's, natural healthy color without need of the sun. Kate allowed herself to briefly wonder about Ellen O'Neil's "roommate," as Taylor had termed her. She said, "That's why I want you to take your time with your answers, Miss O'Neil. Give them thought, reflection. Something may have registered in your mind that you've simply forgotten, something obvious, like Judy Markham. And at the present time you're our single witness, the only source we have."

"All right," she murmured, chastened.

"Go on, Miss O'Neil."

"I took the elevator up. The first elevator as you come into the lobby," she added, attempting a grin.

Oh God she is so like Anne, Kate thought wrenchingly, and closed her eyes for a moment against her pain. "Back up a moment. Was there anyone in the building lobby? Anyone at all?" She watched Ellen O'Neil bend her head over her lap in thought, the soft dark hair separating into currents of subtle browns.

"No. No one."

"What about the guard?"

"There was no guard. The first time I saw Rick and Mike was when they came up on the elevator to get me."

Ellen O'Neil had lifted her head; her gaze was direct, the voice quavery but decisive. "Go on," Kate said. "You got off the elevator."

"I stayed out there for a minute or two, just looking around."

"What did you look at? Describe it to me as well as you can."

Kate held up a hand twice to slow her as she made meticulous shorthand notes of descriptions of furniture and color and fabric; she would check the accuracy of Ellen O'Neil's memory from these notes. Some women pay attention to the damnedest things, she thought; they can describe the most intricate weave in a fabric... She asked, "Did you smell anything?"

"Not that I remember," she said after a moment.

"Perfume? Men's cologne?"

"No. Men's cologne I'd remember. I don't like it."

"I don't either," Kate said with a smile. "Go on."

Ellen was surprised by the smile—magnetically attractive on Kate Delafield's strong face—and surprised by the remark, which made her seem not nearly so bloodless. "I went back to my office—"

"How much time had elapsed by now?" Kate interrupted. "Since you parked your car?" She watched Ellen O'Neil raise both hands, slender, prettier than Anne's, and touch to her temples long fingers tipped with clear polish.

"Three or four minutes."

"Okay. So now it's seven twenty-five. Go on."

As Ellen O'Neil reviewed each move she had made, Kate drew dotted lines on the drawings in her notebook. She tapped her Flair pen on her sketch of the conference room. "Why did you stop here? Why take the long way back around to the kitchen?"

Memory formed vividly in Ellen's mind of her introduction to Fergus Parker. He had leaned back in his immense leather chair, lifted a fat black shiny shoe to one corner of his black slab of a desk, then inserted a black cigar between his wide thick lips, clicking flame from a gold lump of a lighter, holding the cigar between porcine fingers, jowls quivering as he puffed clouds of odoriferous smoke at her. His voice had rumbled out of a chest ringed in fat and encased in a pale yellow suede vest. But she had not heard his words, only seen his eyes: gray and protruding and fixed on her, fixed precisely between her legs.

"Well," Ellen said to Kate Delafield, "I, uh, don't know my way around the office yet."

Kate noted her hesitation and said mildly, "Understandable. But still, why retrace your steps? Why not just continue?"

The hell with it, Ellen decided. "Well, to tell you the truth—"

"Please do."

She doesn't give an inch. In irritation Ellen met the dispassionate blue eyes shaped somewhat like Stephanie's.

Irritation intensified at the thought of Stephanie. *Damn her, treating me like some powder puff excuse for a woman…* "I didn't want to run into Fergus Parker," she stated. "I didn't want to risk being alone with him."

The ever-charming Fergus Parker, Kate thought. "I understand you met him only yesterday."

Ellen said dourly, "With some men it doesn't take long." When Kate smiled, the unexpectedness of it again warmed her.

Indicating with her pen on the sketch, Kate said, "So you came back along this way to your office, down the north corridor …Did you smell anything?"

"Coffee. Just as I got to the kitchen."

"The coffee pot, Miss O'Neil. Concentrate. Picture it as you walked into the kitchen, as you walked over to pour yourself a cup. How full was the pot? How much coffee was left?"

She touched the slim fingers again to her temples. "Better than half."

"Which means how many cups would you say were gone?"

She sighed, thinking, her unseeing eyes on the green-gold painting covering the wall behind Kate. "Well, Styrofoam cups, maybe four. Two or so, if you're filling a mug."

"But a person could make half a pot, isn't that true? Wouldn't someone be more likely to do that early in the morning when no one else was due in till eight o'clock?"

"Not with that kind of coffee maker." She was decisive. "The coffee's premeasured. And the pot of water you put in to make the coffee doesn't make that same pot, but the one after it."

Pleased, Kate paused to complete several notes. "Now, you walked out into the hallway carrying the coffee pot, thinking Guy Adams was in. Why did you think so?"

"Since there were only two offices I hadn't walked past, and the rest of the office doors were closed, that left him and Fergus Parker. And I didn't think Fergus Parker would make coffee." It occurred to her that she had lost personal awareness of Kate Delafield. What was going on had nothing to do with either of them as lesbians.

Kate tapped her pen on her sketch. "What about these people in word processing? You didn't walk past this room. Any of them could be in, couldn't they?"

"Well, yes. Possibly. If they got here early for some reason. But Gail told me yesterday their overtime is pre-approved by him. And one of my duties is to send overtime reports daily by teletype to Philadelphia. He approved overtime yesterday for only two people in credit who had to work last night."

"But someone could have been in there."

"Someone could have been in any of the offices. Working behind a closed door."

"Was Guy Adams' door closed?"

"Uh, yes." She bit her lips; her response had been pure impulse.

Kate looked at her in surprise. Training and experience, every instinct told her Ellen O'Neil was lying. The eye shift. The change in facial set, vocal intonation. And she had been unprepared for the question, had not taken enough time to consider it if she were genuinely uncertain. Kate watched her, allowing silence to accumulate.

What did Guy have to do with this, Ellen thought. Why should I put him through all this? Why should I give that dear man a problem?

Kate thought: She's looking at me the way people do when they're lying. Why in God's name would she want to protect Guy Adams? Maybe Taylor's wrong about her and her roommate. Maybe they're just that, roommates. "How long have you known Mr. Adams?"

"Just since yesterday, of course."

Belligerence had been in the tone. Hesitating, Kate looked down at her notes. Her training told her to bring all the weight of her authority upon Ellen O'Neil's stiffening resistance, back her into a corner, suggest—no, threaten—a charge of obstruction of justice, of perjury. That worked with the majority of witnesses in the world of crime and criminals, and certainly would work here in Amateur City, as Taylor had termed it. It would also change— chill—her tenuous relationship with this woman, a witness with a strong appearance of honesty and credibility if and when a case was put together to present for prosecution. She would come back to Guy Adams; perhaps later Ellen O'Neil would correct her story voluntarily. Strictly a judgment call, she told herself.

A scrupulous inner voice asked, is it a judgment call, or are you avoiding confrontation because she reminds you of Anne?

She said, "What made you first think something was wrong?"

"Thudding sounds, vibration under my feet from somebody running. A door slamming. Loudly."

Ellen O'Neil had shifted in her chair with the new direction of the question, and Kate noted the easing of her posture. "At what point did you hear the thudding? Where were you exactly in the hallway?"

"Right outside Guy's office." Ellen sat up again, remembering that she had been looking at that moment through Guy's window at the green of the mountains, the mist over the ocean.

"And the slamming door?"

"The same. It was only a few seconds later."

"I see. What did you do then?"

"Nothing. It came from Fergus Parker's direction, so I figured it was his office door and none of my business."

"But did you move at all? Where were you in the hallway? Had you gone back toward the kitchen?"

She concentrated. "I might have taken a step in that direction. But then I heard glass breaking and I ran down the hall."

"Ran?"

"I was carrying the coffee pot, but I moved as fast as I could. I slowed up as I got to his office."

Deliberately, Kate stared at her. Then she said, injecting a note of cold skepticism into her tone, "You decided not to investigate thudding feet and a slamming door but yet you *ran* down the hall because glass was breaking?"

Those ice-blue eyes—like being on a skewer. Does she think I'm making this up, for God's sake? "Look, the noise was so *loud.* There was a kind of...I don't know, *violence* to the way it was smashing, like something awful was happening."

"Something awful *was* happening," Kate said quietly, seizing the moment. "A man was dying. Miss O'Neil, have you left anything out that you heard or saw in that hallway? Anything?"

Ellen hesitated; the blue eyes held hers, the voice was compelling. But anything she said now would only compound matters, and Guy had been so kind to her... "That's all I can remember now," she said. "But I'll give it—give everything more thought."

"Good." The moment was gone, but the answer had been temporizing. "What happened next?"

Tears sprang to Ellen O'Neil's eyes. Kate allowed her to speak uninterrupted, not taking notes; she listened without moving to the details of discovering the body; the realization that a killer might be anywhere on the floor; her actions in the lobby; the arrival of the guards. As Ellen O'Neil described the two guards backing toward her with guns drawn and then the descent to safety on the elevator, her voice broke.

"Many people—most people—would have screamed, run in panic, perhaps—probably—gotten themselves killed." Kate spoke slowly, turning and smoothing pages of her notes to allow Ellen O'Neil time. She had always considered her lack of reaction to tears an advantage she held over male detectives, most of whom dissolved in the presence of a sobbing woman, and conversely treated a sobbing man with cold contempt. Tears were a healthy manifestation, that was all; she envied anyone, male or female, who could do something she could not do at all. "In most crimes of murder," she said, "the killer will protect himself at all cost. You handled yourself with the kind of presence of mind we teach to police officers."

Flushing with the pleasure of a compliment from this forbidding woman, Ellen murmured, "Thank you." Then she stared as Kate Delafield buried her face in her hands and took a deep shuddering breath, ran her hands through the graying hair. Could she be suffering from some illness?

Like a swimmer coming up from a depth and gasping for air, Kate surfaced from the agony of memory—Anne's face flushed after lovemaking. "Miss O'Neil?" Her voice seemed to echo in her chest. "I know this has been very difficult. But would you show me in the office what you've described to me?"

"Of course," Ellen said gently.

They went into the lobby, through the far doors and into Ellen's office, then down the corridor. Ellen paused before Matt Bradford's office. "I came in here first."

A balding portly man, jacketless, a well-loosened tie hanging from the unbuttoned collar of a white shirt, was bent over his desk examining blueprints. He did not look up. Kate took Ellen's arm and led her along the corridor.

"Miss O'Neil, Matt Bradford's office. Was it open?"

"Yes, but he wasn't in yesterday and it was open all day."

"Do you know why?"

She shook her head. Kate jotted a notation to ask Gail Freeman.

"Then I looked in here." She pushed open the door to Customer Service and Credit.

"Hi Cagney!" shrieked Judy Markham.

Activity halted; a sea of faces turned up to them. People nudged one another, pointed. Ellen stepped back, let the door swing shut.

"Jesus," she whispered.

Kate said calmly, "Who was it that predicted everyone'd be famous for twenty minutes?"

"Andy Warhol," Ellen answered automatically, still stunned by the staring faces.

"In a day or two everything will be back to normal. Try not to let that part bother you. Let's go on."

Kate verified a few notes as they walked slowly past open offices, and she looked in. Fred Grayson glanced up, then bent over his work. Harley Burton's office was empty. Duane Fletcher, broad yellow-shirted back turned to them, hands behind his bald head, sat with his feet up on his credenza and stared out the window. Gretchen Phillips talked on the phone in low calm tones as she searched through mounds of paper burying her desk.

Billie Sullivan passed them with her dipping, loping gait, stringy carrot-colored hair swaying. She had added a new element to her costume of khaki skirt and fuzzy aqua sweater: her legs were covered by ripply gray leg warmers.

"That's Billie Sullivan," Ellen said, chuckling at the amazement on Kate Delafield's face.

"Yes, I know." Kate watched Billie Sullivan until she vanished around a corner. "Unreal."

Remembering the events of this day, Ellen said soberly, "Gail wants to fire her."

"Yes, he told me," Kate said thoughtfully. Billie Sullivan could be an interesting interview. Perhaps two interviews—one before, one after her termination.

At the conference room Ellen said, "I came only this far."

Kate glanced back down the hallway, then walked toward Fergus Parker's office at the end of the corridor, to a lighted EXIT sign; she pulled open the heavy metal-weighted door that led to a staircase, let it swing shut, cushioning the momentum with pressure from her foot. She moved briskly across to Fergus Parker's office, pacing off the distance.

The door of the executive washroom was flung open and Harley Burton strode into the hall, rolling down the sleeves of his chalk white shirt. He nodded curtly as he came toward her; she felt pierced by his dark stare. He continued down the corridor toward his office. She heard Ellen murmur a greeting and Harley Burton's gruff-voiced rejoinder.

They retraced their steps, Ellen moving impatiently ahead, past Gail Freeman who was on the phone and tossed Kate a mock-military salute in passing. In the kitchen, Ellen reconstructed her actions of the morning, pouring coffee and then carrying the styrofoam cup and a half-filled coffee pot into the hallway toward Guy Adams' office.

Ellen smiled; Guy sat at his desk gesturing emphatically to a thin young woman with mountainous frizzy hair. He glimpsed Ellen and rose, murmuring apology to his visitor, and walked into the hallway.

"Ellen, is everything all right? Are you okay?"

Tension in the voice, thought Kate. And the way he stares at her...

"Is there anything I can do?" He had directed his question at Kate, then focused his gaze again on Ellen O'Neil.

Perhaps tense by nature, Kate thought. And he seems totally

smitten by her... "I'll have questions for you later, Mr. Adams." When he did not move she added in a tone of dismissal, "Now if you'll excuse us."

Obediently, Guy Adams walked into his office, but remained just over the threshold, looking on. Kate said, "Miss O'Neil, I want you to tell me if what you hear is what you heard this morning."

Ellen turned to face Guy's office as she had that morning, then glanced back to see Kate Delafield walking down the corridor, straight and trim in her gray pants and corduroy jacket, her walk compact and purposeful. "I was facing this way," she said in a low tone to Guy. "As I recall, your office door was closed."

She searched his face; his green eyes stared dully into hers. She turned away to look down the hallway. Perhaps he doesn't know it was open, she thought; maybe he doesn't even remember.

Kate had reached the lobby door. She pulled it fully open, released it. Cushioned by an air brake, it closed with stately progress, securing itself with a solid *thunk*.

"Much louder than that," Ellen called.

Kate walked across to Fergus Parker's office, grasped the doorknob, slammed the door violently.

Ellen walked part way down the hall. "It was loud like that, but not quite so close, you made the floor vibrate under my feet. I didn't feel that before, only from the footsteps. And besides, that door was wide open when I got to it.

Reflecting, Kate absently shifted the holster chafing her hip under her jacket. "The killer might've started to come out, spotted you, slammed the door in panic. Then decided you might come anyway, so he opened it again and hid behind it, waiting."

Ellen O'Neil shuddered, and Kate said quickly, "It's very unlikely, that scenario. There'd be no reason for him to open the door again. He'd be more likely to wait with it closed."

Ellen sipped coffee, calming herself and thinking. "Well, no. He might think he'd be more helpless that way, he'd have to judge when to come out and I might see him and escape, there might be someone else on the floor by now to help me. And the way Fergus Parker was killed, I don't know if he'd even have another weapon, unless it was a bludgeon of some kind."

Disagreeing with her, Kate nodded in respect for her logic. "Possible. But doubtful a killer would act so deliberately and coolly after committing such a crime. Natural instinct would almost certainly compel him to run. Miss O'Neil, I'd like to try something else. Would you go back to where you were before?"

She waited until Ellen had again stationed herself outside Guy Adams' office. Adams stood in his doorway still looking on, his frizzy-haired visitor gone. Kate walked around the corner toward the conference room and the EXIT stairway. She pulled the EXIT fire door fully open, released it. Accumulating rapid momentum, the door hit the jamb with an echoing thunder of sound.

"That's it! That's it!" Ellen O'Neil shouted.

Kate glimpsed movement; Gretchen Phillips popped out of her doorway, then as swiftly vanished into her office. As Kate rounded the corner of the hallway, Ellen was trotting awkwardly toward her cradling the coffee pot.

"I'm positive that's what it was. The stairway door?"

"Right. Here, let me take the coffee pot." Kate smiled. "I won't need you to show me how you dropped it." She was pleased when Ellen O'Neil laughed.

"The killer ran down the stairs, then?"

"Probably. Exited in the garage, I would think."

"But sixteen floors? How would he have enough time? Rick and Mike said—"

"Excuse me." Gail Freeman had come up to them. "All the info you want, all the files are locked in the conference room." He tossed a key to Kate, who deftly caught it in her free hand. "They're confidential."

Kate pocketed the key. "I'll see they're properly safe-guarded." She glanced at her watch. "Miss O'Neil, I'll have further questions. Let's say one-thirty. In the conference room." She turned to Gail Freeman. "If Detective Taylor is looking for me, I'll be with Mr. Grayson."

Ellen watched admiringly until Kate Delafield disappeared around the corner of the corridor.

Chapter 4

Kate looked around slowly, amazed by the lackluster furnishings in the large corner office of Fred Grayson, senior sales manager of Modern Office, Inc. The prosaic square sofa and armchairs were of matching beige corduroy; a plain walnut coffee table matched two lamp tables; the pale blue lamps also matched. Books in groups of three or four were clustered between wood-block bookends, photographs huddled in small groups on the vast expanses of wall. A tiny table with a philodendron trailing from it had been placed indecisively along one wall; a number of sharp leg marks were visible and recent in the carpeting. On the credenza behind Fred Grayson, who sat at a massive oak desk, was a carefully posed photograph of a brown-haired woman perched at the far end of a beige sofa, three children stiffly erect beside her in descending order of height.

Fred Grayson puffed on a small cigar, a fine sprinkle of ash falling onto his dark green tie and over his desk blotter. "I'm surprised as hell you're letting people go in and out, even out to lunch."

Kate took out her notebook. "Not much choice. We can't keep people cooped up when we're still developing and evaluating background."

Fred Grayson raised bushy brown-gray eyebrows. "Well," he said.

The word had been said in two drawn-out syllables, the insinuation almost comical. "Any information you might have could be valuable," Kate encouraged. "Might even catch us a killer."

Grayson adjusted his horn rims, puffed on his little cigar, surveyed her. "My nephew's wife, she's in police work, maybe you know her? Denise Grayson. Pasadena. She's in, uh, traffic enforcement."

Meter maid, Kate thought. "Afraid not. I've never worked that division. With almost seven thousand of us in law enforcement—"

"Sure." Grayson nodded additional emphasis. "Denise's a little thing—bright girl, I'll concede that. She's talking more and more about a police career now that the politics of these times have forced the standards so much lower."

Kate looked at Grayson, and remained silent.

"Don't mean you of course," Grayson said hurriedly, his glance sliding away. "At least you're a decent height, what, five-eight? And look like you handle yourself fine. Not that I'd ever need that kind of help, but I'd sure hate to have one of these new five-foot lady cops try and bail me out of a tough situation."

"She wouldn't try," Kate said mildly, assessing the wide shoulders under the green striped shirt, the bulging biceps. "Every major police department today has trained teams for things like that. But if she did help, you might be surprised. In a contest with even a good-sized man, training can make all the difference."

"Too dangerous a line of work for women," Fred Grayson declared.

Kate shrugged. Why waste time trying to raise the consciousness of a person like Fred Grayson? But she said, "It's cop shows that promote the idea of danger. All the police in L.A. put together don't fire as many shots in a year as they do in some of those shows. The mortality rate's higher in many other professions. Mining. Construction. Even agriculture."

"I read all the time about you cops getting shot."

"From ambush, almost always. And it doesn't matter then whether you're five feet tall or seven feet tall. But there's accumulating evidence to suggest that the presence of women actually helps some situations—" Fred Grayson's scowl was deepening. He had hinted at information he possessed; she would lead him back to this subject.

"My nephew," Grayson said heavily, "he's not about to let Denise ever get into a situation like that. Little thing that she is, she ought to have more damn sense."

Kate chose her words, deciding to skirt the edge of hypocrisy. "Decisions like that are up to the people best informed and most directly involved, don't you think?"

"Damn right." Fred Grayson adjusted his glasses again. "Now don't misunderstand, I don't discriminate—"

"Mr. Grayson," Kate said impatiently, then paused to soften her tone. "You have information relevant to this investigation?"

"Say anything today somebody hollers discrimination," Grayson continued doggedly. "People misunderstand, you know." He was looking at her intently, hazel eyes owlish behind the thick lenses. "Tell somebody a damn *fact* about some minority group and they holler stereotype. They holler *bigot.*"

Understanding, Kate sat comfortably back in her chair, resisting an urge to lift an ankle to her knee. This was familiar ground. She smiled. "I may be a woman, but nobody's ever given me anything. I've worked for everything I have. And it's a statistical fact who's responsible for most crime in our fair city."

Fred Grayson beamed. "By God it's good to meet somebody who understands. Somebody you can talk to, not one of those bleeding hearts…I put stock in statistics, myself, you know."

"Somebody was knocking statistics to me just last week. Said just because the tables say a man's life expectancy's sixty-five doesn't mean he won't live a day beyond." Kate chuckled; she was enjoying herself.

Fred Grayson's thick eyebrows almost met in a fierce beetling. He gestured with his cigar, dropping ash. "People know *shit* about statistics, they *always* argue with crap like that. Excuse my language but—"

Wanting to deemphasize the male-female aspects of this interview, Kate interrupted, "Forget the language. You can't say anything I haven't heard and plenty more." Abruptly she switched direction, saying bluntly, "You've got what, five, six blacks? A few Latinos?"

"The three beaners are okay. Quiet, mind their own business, aren't trying to take over the company. But the coons …" Puffing out an enormous cloud of smoke, he watched Kate. "Pardon me, I believe in calling a spade a spade."

Deliberately, Kate smiled. Grayson laughed, slapping his desk with heavy thwacks of a thick-fingered hand. "Good to meet somebody that understands," he repeated. "Cops, it takes cops to know the real world. We got five coons here in the office, two more outside. One's insolent as hell, the inky bastard. Works for Duane, southeast territory, no self-respecting white man'd ever take that territory. Gretchen's got one too, a cu—a woman named Cassie Franklin." He looked meaningfully at Kate's notebook. "I see you take a lot of notes. Important, what I'm telling you?"

"Good notes are very important in a case of homicide. You're telling me you think the black employees are involved?"

"Come on, Fergus was stabbed. You cops know how the jungle bunnies like knives. Niggers love cutting up whitey."

Kate turned to a fresh page in the back of her notebook and wrote four words, and looked up to see Grayson gazing at her in satisfaction. She said, "You know statistics and suspicion never got anyone arrested."

"Sure, I'm not that stupid. I got a top suspect for you. The head nigger."

"Mr. Grayson, I'm not totally familiar with your organization, your personnel—"

Grayson said impatiently, "The guy you were with in the hallway, the spade with the girl's name. The nigger they pushed into the wrong goddamn job." Grayson jabbed his cigar at a metal ashtray; ash teetered on the edge, fell onto the desk.

"Does Gail Freeman do a poor job?"

"Listen. A man in my position, I *need* a secretary. Before he got here, I *had* a secretary. Then he…reorganized." The word dripped acid. "He said Helen wasn't…productive." He seized the ashtray; sparks leaped onto the desk as he stabbed the life from his cigar. "So now he's got her in that damn big room back there. Working with Christ knows what all, Filipinos, niggers. Some Jap supervisor tells her what to do. Helen hates it."

"That's too bad," Kate said evenly. "But what motive would Freeman have for wanting Fergus Parker dead?"

"Hate, pure and simple. Hated his guts. The nigger reports to Philadelphia, you know. So Fergus couldn't get him fired. But he made that coon's life miserable. Argued every capital equipment item he asked for, every change he made in the office. But those damn fools back East, they want these damn computers, they love these damn word processors. Everything's in the computer today. A man can't even have his girl open a file drawer and take out a damn piece of paper. Don't get me wrong, computers are okay. Amazing, I'll even say. But the fun's gone. Time was you could bullshit, wing it. If you guessed right, you'd make yourself look like a hero when the year-end numbers came out. Nowadays you do that and some pissant kid that doesn't even shave, he's gonna punch his pocket calculator and make you look like fresh shit from Mrs. Astor's horse—"

"I'm investigating a murder," Kate interrupted, bored and exasperated. "I need an adequate motive for murder. People don't kill people they hate. Or," she added with a covert, baleful glance at Fred Grayson, "most of us would be dead."

"I was getting to it," Grayson said in an injured tone. "We were in the coon's office, Fergus and me. About the coon's latest brainstorm, he wanted to knock down a lobby wall, make more room for those flunkies in the service bay. Modular work areas, can you believe it? We need a lobby, for chrissake. Imagine our customers coming in to buy office interiors and we've got this dinky little lobby all because bright boy—"

"Mr. Grayson," Kate said coldly.

"I was just trying to show you how he thinks, our *efficient* office manager." Grayson glared at her, thick fingers drumming on the desk. He fumbled in the drawer, took out a package of Tiparillos. "You smoke at all?"

"Not for years. My—I gave it up."

"Wife's been after me. I switch off to these things once in a while. They taste like horseshit. But somebody like Fergus dies, only forty-eight, you realize…" He extracted a cigar, inspected it, inserted it between his fleshy lips, fumbled in another drawer for matches.

Kate shifted, and no longer caring about Grayson's opinion, lifted an ankle onto a knee, reflecting blackly that men in power always inflicted petty tyrannies, always arrogantly assumed no one's time could be as valuable as their own.

"Story's kind of funny, really." Grayson puffed on his thin cigar. "Like I said, we were in the head nigger's office, arguing, and Fergus's warning him not to use Guy as a go-between like he did wasting money on that word processing room, which is another story. Then Fergus gets up and walks around and picks up the picture of the coon's family. 'Pretty woman,' Fergus says, 'pretty daughters. Makes me think of the first time I ever went to bed with a black woman.' See? Fergus is being nice and proper, using all the proper words, not saying the words he usually would, like—well, you know. So this coon can't take offense, know what I mean?"

Kate, writing in her notebook, nodded response.

"Looked a lot like Marian,' Fergus says. Marian's Mrs. Coon. 'Same size tits,' Fergus said. 'Built just like Marian, too. Loved it, she did. Said she just loved a white man doing it to her.' See how Fergus was going on?"

"Yes," Kate said.

"Then Fergus says, 'This's your older daughter, right? Pauline, isn't that her name?' Fergus was always good about names. And the coon nods, his Adams apple's bobbing up and down from swallowing, he's staring at Fergus, eyes about popping out of his head. 'I had one just about exactly her age too,' Fergus says. 'Did it to her doggy-style. She said she liked it that way best from a white man.' " Grayson brayed laughter. "And Fergus went on and on, I won't go into all the detail, you can figure it out. Ever see a spook turn white, Detective? This spook was white under that shit-colored skin. This coon was a puddle on the floor. And Fergus strolled out, and I followed him, but I hung back a little and peeked around the corner and this coon was standing there rigid as a post and saying 'I'll kill him I'll kill him I'll kill him...' "

Kate asked, "When was this?"

"Friday. You think the spook had enough motive?"

Kate finished her notes and added another word to the page in the back of her book. "Yes," she said.

"Thought so," Grayson said.

"What was your relationship to the victim?"

Fred Grayson's eyebrows beetled again. "Meaning...like what?"

"It's a simple question, Mr. Grayson. Were you friendly? Cordial? Or did you have a business relationship? Or was it cooler than that?"

"Of those choices," Grayson said, looking at her warily, "a business relationship."

"From what I understand, Fergus Parker was detested around here."

"A man in my position doesn't make friends in the office. Fergus Parker was one management level above me." Grayson puffed on his cigar. "Draw your own conclusions."

"No friends, that's one thing. Outright hatred is something else."

Grayson studied his cigar, adjusted his horn rims. "His style was...well, he didn't care about being liked. He must've...I think he worked at not being liked. Him and his damn tests—"

"What tests?"

"If you argued, protested something he'd done, he'd look at you like you just shot his mother. Then he'd tell you he'd been testing you and you'd just failed... It was a stinking little game of his, to make you afraid of him. I think he thought fear made him effective, gained him respect—"

"Did you respect him?"

"No," Grayson said immediately.

"Did he ever do anything to you?"

Grayson stared at Kate, opened his mouth, closed it firmly, stubbed out his cigar and looked away. "Lots of his...tests. Nothing I can think of specifically."

Lying, she knew. "Did any other employee other than Mr. Freeman have reason to harm Mr. Parker?"

"Harm him?" Grayson's bray of laughter ended abruptly. "Break both his legs if they thought they could do it some way and get away with it. Fergus stomped everybody. A game, like I said, a game ... Me thinking that, it's the only thing that made some of it...tolerable."

Kate asked with light irony, "Can you name individuals who might not have reached your state of tolerance?"

"Like I said, Fergus stomped everybody. But he didn't dislike everybody, if you get the difference. Except for the coon. And Guy Adams. Called him a fag all the time."

She asked with interest, remembering Guy Adams' too friendly handshake, his staring at Ellen O'Neil, "Is he?"

Grayson shrugged. "Sometimes he seems a little faggy. But I think he's okay. And I never heard that from anybody else, just Fergus." He added with a challenging glare, "But he'd never make a pass at me, now would he?"

"I doubt it," she said drily. "Anyone else Fergus Parker did things to?"

Grayson picked up a memo from his desk in an unsubtle hint that he wished to return to his work. "Let me think about it, get back to you."

Politics, she guessed. Except for Gail Freeman and Guy Adams there could be political consequences if he named anyone else. "I'm investigating a homicide," she said, stressing the words and tapping her pen on her notebook in an unsubtle reminder that the business at hand took precedence. "I don't think I have to tell you that withholding of any information by any individual regardless of his motivation is obstruction of justice."

Grayson's bushy eyebrows met. He slammed down the memo. "I'm not obstructing justice, goddammit. I'm just telling you I have to think about it."

She pulled a card from the pocket of her notebook, tossed it onto the desk. "One more question," she said as Grayson slid the card into his shirt pocket. "What time did you arrive this morning?"

Grayson glared at her. "Why? You think I've got something to do with this?"

"At this point I don't think anything. I'm gathering facts."

"Well, I gave you a pretty good lead, didn't I?"

"Remains to be seen. All the information you supply will be given the attention it deserves. Please answer my question."

"About ten to eight. Cops all over the place. Couldn't get in the lobby or upstairs for one hell of a long time."

"Were other company employees there?"

"The head nigger. Acting like Mr. Bigshot rounding everybody up, taking charge. He got the guards to open up that insurance company down there, he herded everybody in. Except for me. He wasn't about to tell Fred Grayson—"

"Mr. Grayson," she said, barely controlling her impatience, "just answer my question. At ten minutes to eight, who exactly did you see?"

"Just watch your tone there, lady detective. I'm a taxpaying citizen, a damn good taxpaying citizen. I don't have to take any crap from any—"

"I'm doing my job, Mr. Grayson, as efficiently as possible. I have many more interviews after yours. If you'd prefer to give your information to another investigator, I'll have an officer take you to the station."

"Oh shit. Come on, let's back off, okay? I've got a short fuse."

She did not reply; she waited with Flair pen poised.

"What was the question?"

She did not answer.

"Who did I see, that it? The head nigger, Guy Adams. Matt, Matt Bradford. I was glad to see him, I needed to—" Grayson met Kate's upward glance and said hurriedly, "Judy with the big tits, I don't know her last name, the receptionist. Gretchen was there, cracking jokes. We didn't know what was going on yet and she said she bet they were arresting Fergus Parker for indecent exposure which in his case would be a felony."

Grayson chuckled; Kate understood that he was trying to be ingratiating. She smiled. "Anyone else?"

"Harley, I mentioned Harley, didn't I? And Duane. Some of those people in the back bay, the Jap supervisor in word processing, I can give you first names is all."

"Whatever."

"Uh, Ralph. Bill. They're service people in the back bay. John, he's in credit. Betty, she's word processing. I don't know the Jap supervisor's name. That's all I can remember right now."

"How long have you had your present position, Mr. Grayson?"

"Seven years," Grayson said proudly. "Came out of St. Louis. Been in this corner office four months. Harley used to have it. That's Harley Burton next door. You plan on talking to him?"

"Yes. Of course. Why do you ask?"

Grayson sighed. "Might not have many good things to say about me. I took his job, his office."

"I'm investigating a murder, not office politics," she said curtly. But she made a note. The demotion of Harley Burton probably would have been Fergus Parker's decision. She rose. "Mr. Grayson, let me know if you remember any other facts relevant to this case."

"Sure." Grayson got to his feet, leaned over the desk to shake hands, sat down and again picked up the memo.

In the hallway, Kate glanced at the page in the back of her notebook and the five words she had written: Coon. Spade. Jungle bunny. Nigger. Spook.

"Left out jigaboo," she murmured, and flipped the notebook closed. Lunch, she thought, I could really use a break.

Chapter 5

Ellen's mother said, "So I had to hear the news from the *perfessor*. Are you sure you're all right? Why didn't you call me?"

"I haven't had time, they've been questioning me. I'm fine, Mother." Ellen shifted the receiver to the other ear, picturing her mother in the customary pink robe, sitting amid the orange and yellow floral pillows of her sofa, platinum hair in curlers as it always was until early afternoon; soon she would comb out the hair, don culottes and a jersey top, and venture out of her Valley apartment with the *Times* under her arm to pass the afternoon with her poolside neighbors.

"You're incredible," her mother said, "you and the perfessor." She had always called Stephanie that, always pronouncing the word sarcastically. "So what was it like, darling?" Her voice lowered dramatically. "Tell me all about it."

"I found a man with a knife in his chest."

"Dear, oh dear. Why ever are you still there?"

"Mother, murder isn't a normal part of their daily routine here."

"Don't be disrespectful. There's a murderer on the loose, maybe right there with you. That wonderful intelligent perfessor told me she's leaving town tonight anyway. I know I don't understand the life you lead, but how she can leave you alone at a time like this—"

"Dammit, Mother—"

"Well, they haven't arrested anybody yet, have they?"

"I'm sure they will soon. The detective in charge, she seems very good at her work, very tough and capable—"

"A woman detective? In charge? A tough and capable *woman?* What's happening to this world? Where have all the men gone? Why couldn't you find yourself a tough and capable man instead of this other craziness in your head? Or even a tough and capable woman, if it has to be that. Anybody who wouldn't drape herself all over you, drain you dry—"

Ellen sighed, cradled the receiver between her shoulder and ear, began to sort the mail. Her mother had managed to accept her lesbianism only by taking refuge in the belief that some day Ellen would recover from it.

"Two years of college, you're educated—a bright girl, darling. But one part of your head—it's that marijuana, you can't tell me you don't smoke it, all people your age do. Why can't you drink gin? Or even scotch? Like a normal person? First it's Lydia the bum and seven years to come to your senses, then this perfessor—"

Out of patience, Ellen said firmly, "Mother, take it to the cleaners."

"I don't like it, a murder where you work and you all alone in that apartment, I'm worried about you, darling. And I was going out tonight but instead I think I'll—"

"You go right ahead and go out, Mother. I mean it. This isn't an episode of *The A Team*. I'm hardly an eyewitness anyone needs to knock off. I didn't see a thing. So there's no reason to—"

"Even so, it's a crazy world we live in, full of John Hinckleys and Pope killers—"

Ellen changed the subject. "Who are you going out with? The one with the wrist watch that plays *The Yellow Rose of Texas?*"

"Yes. Sam, who wants to marry me. And be nice to your poor mother who only loves you and wants you to be married."

"A diabetic recommending sugar," Ellen twitted. Her mother had been married five times; Ellen's Irish father had been husband number two.

"I'm still right. You and that perfessor, you're so far off base—"

"Mother, would you really be happier if I were miserably married to some man?"

"I was brought up in a generation that believed we take on responsibilities in life, and—"

Ellen sighed again. "Mother, I'm a child of a freer generation. You're a child of yours."

"Bullcrap," said her mother.

Ellen glimpsed baggy leg warmers, a fuzzy aqua sweater; Billie Sullivan loped by, sandwich in hand. "Mother, I have to go to lunch now."

Coming out of the kitchen with a cellophaned ham salad sandwich, she saw Kate Delafield down the hallway just outside Guy Adams' office. She also had a sandwich, and stood talking to the detective who had questioned Ellen earlier—Ed Taylor, she remembered.

Kate Delafield was very trim, about five-eight, she judged, younger than Taylor—perhaps late thirties—and more conservative in bearing and dress. Her solid body was straight, and she wore a simple open-throat white blouse with her green corduroy jacket and gray slacks. Taylor, beefy shoulders slouched, wore a suit of brown checks, a blue shirt, a wide tie of blues and yellows. Kate Delafield gestured impatiently with a compact, kinetic motion of her arm; Taylor listened, head bent, shifting his bulk from one foot to the other. Kate Delafield walked off, around the corner, Taylor following.

Ellen returned to her office, ate her sandwich at her desk. She thought about the faces she knew at Modern Office, scarcely familiar faces—strangers. Her mother's melodramatics notwithstanding, a killer knew who she was, that she had been here this morning... She told herself there was no reason for fear. But it would be good if someone was arrested, and soon.

Taylor said, "The people I'm talking to, clerks, service reps, they're just the peons. I'm trying to get the gossip, get a line on somebody who really had it in for this bird."

"Good idea, Ed." Kate had finished the recap of her morning, and she and Taylor were walking toward the conference room.

"But Christ, Kate. Nothing but garbage so far. Betty-somebody lives with a wop, every full moon he beats the living shit out of her. Bill-somebody's got a wife that bets both their paychecks in the Gardena poker parlors—"

"Why in God's name do good people stay with rotten people?" Kate said, striding into the conference room.

"Beats me. Marie ever did anything like that, they'd have to scrape up the pieces."

Kate said drily, "You wouldn't consider just leaving her?"

"Yeah, that too." Taylor threw his notebook onto the conference room table. "Mabel-somebody, she guzzles gin out of her thermos all day long, Fred-somebody, he—"

"Wait a minute. Narcotics. Anybody give you anything at all? Coke? Pills? Grass? Anything at all?"

"You mean somebody stoned could've..." Taylor rubbed his jaw. "Just that weird Sullivan dame, June-somebody told me Billie Sullivan smokes reefers in the john, that's all I've got."

"Watch that angle, Ed. Anything's as possible as anything else till we get a handle."

"Amateur City," Taylor said disgustedly.

Kate unwrapped her sandwich, spread a napkin on the table.

"Kate, come out to lunch, you don't want that machine shit, loaded with all those preservatives. What's an hour for lunch? Whoever did this isn't gonna run. Amateur City, they never run. Let's go eat Chinese, get a beer—"

Taylor's face showed concern. Some of the men Kate worked with, with whom she had never and would never discuss her private life, had shown similar concern over the past months. Through her coating of numbness she had felt their reaching out to her in a common humanity—awkward expressions of caring from men who had seen every kind of grisly horror and had layered themselves with deep protective coats of cynicism. Kate said quietly, "Thanks Ed, I appreciate it. But I want to look through these files, get some background on a few people, save some time."

"Okay. See you later."

She made a swift inspection of the folders Gail Freeman had supplied, pocketed the printout of employees to run a check. Then she propped her feet on a chair, contemplated the soothing greens and yellows of the huge painting covering the opposite wall, picked up half of her sandwich. She reviewed what she had learned so far about the death of Fergus Parker.

The killer was by all odds a Modern Office employee—or a relative of an employee—present or past; entry could not have been gained to the sixteenth floor without possession of a key.

The notation would have been made on the guards' log if anyone had preceded or accompanied Fergus Parker, and the killer could not have remained on the premises the night before without discovery by the guards or cleaning personnel; therefore he or she had arrived between seven and seven-forty, before or after Ellen O'Neil. In all probability, pending verification of Fergus Parker's personal habits, he or she was a current employee who had arrived in time to make and drink coffee.

Robbery was not an apparent motive. There was no evident sign of struggle, no blood smears or splatter. The hands were bloody, but it was the usual involuntary reflex of a victim to clutch at a mortal wound. The damage in the office had been caused by Fergus Parker himself, in the final moments of his life. And he had been murdered by someone he knew, someone he did not fear—he had been totally surprised by the act.

She finished the half of her sandwich, threw the other half into the wastebasket, and pulled the stack of folders toward her. She paused, thinking about Ellen O'Neil. In all good conscience she could no longer be anything but rigorously professional. And that meant taking off the gloves.

Chapter 6

Ellen returned to the conference room. Feeling Kate Delafield's blue eyes on her, she walked self-consciously, awkwardly. She sat down and rubbed her palms over the rough tweed of her skirt.

Without preamble, Kate asked, "Have you reconsidered your statements of this morning, Miss O'Neil?" She had planned her approach, and continued before Ellen O'Neil could respond, "I'll make it easier for you by reconstructing a few facts."

She laced her fingers together and leaned forward on her elbows. "This morning a man—or woman—was in Fergus Parker's office at seven-forty, and for an undetermined length of time before that. For reasons unknown at this point, this person fatally stabbed Fergus Parker. Then this person came out of the office into the hallway."

Kate sat back and pushed Pete Johnson's sketch of the sixteenth floor to the center of the table. "It's my opinion that this person saw you in the hallway, and in that same instant saw that he or she would have to move—" Kate scowled at Johnson's tiny print, "—eighteen feet toward you to exit into the lobby. Therefore, this person gambled on a dash across the hallway, a distance of only—" she scowled again, "—seven feet to the intersecting hallway. In the anxiety for escape, this person then flung the stairway door fully open, causing the slam which we duplicated a while ago, and fled down the stairs."

Kate folded the sketch and fixed her eyes on Ellen O'Neil. "In the meantime, Miss O'Neil, a man was dying. And these are the things we know so far about how he died." Kate brought her hands to her chest. "He instantly clutched at the knife plunged into him. Then he took his hands from his mortal wound and grabbed at the desk to pull himself up." Kate reached to the table in front of her, still staring at Ellen O'Neil. "His slick bloody hands slipped off the desk."

Ellen buried her face in her hands, unable to bear the images.

Kate continued relentlessly, "Then he reached for something he could grasp, the portable bar which was quite near his desk. Perhaps he was able to rise somewhat, perhaps not at all. But he pulled the bar over, causing the enormous crashing of glass which you heard next. Then he turned his chair, tried to reach behind him to the phone on the credenza. Look at me, Miss O'Neil."

Unwillingly, she raised her head, opened her eyes.

Kate sat with her chair turned slightly, arms outstretched as Fergus Parker's arms had been in death. "He managed to turn his chair only a few degrees, to reach out. And you found him just as he died."

Again Ellen buried her face in her hands.

"Please look at me, Miss O'Neil."

Again she raised her head. Kate Delafield sat with arms crossed, elbows resting on the table. Her light blue eyes were not cold, they were not hostile, but they bored into Ellen's as if she were seeing all the way to the back of her head.

"There was a reason why a murderer got across that hallway to safety, why you never saw who it was. Your back was turned. And your back was turned because you were looking into Guy Adams' office. Through his open door into his office." Her voice rose slightly. "Isn't that true?"

"Yes," she whispered, "it's true."

Kate said with a hint of a smile, "I'm not that clever." She flipped open the sketch. "Officer Johnson drew the main features of the sixteenth floor soon after the premises were secured. His sketch shows Mr. Adams' door open."

With difficulty, Ellen managed a smile. Then she said venomously, "Where did you learn your questioning technique, the KGB?"

Kate chuckled. "Maybe law school. I went for a year." Anxious to reestablish cordiality, she pushed the sketch and her notes aside, away from Ellen O'Neil's direct view, and smiled again.

"Really?" Anger faded; Kate Delafield seemed suddenly more accessible, and Ellen was interested and curious. "Why did you quit?"

"Criminal law was the one aspect that appealed to me. But I learned I wouldn't be comfortable on either side, defending or convicting."

"Why? I don't understand."

"I started law school in 'seventy-nine when women were finally being allowed into the more challenging areas of police work. By then I'd advanced far enough in my work to realize there was little appeal in spending my energy and ingenuity defending a possible criminal. The other choice was prosecution—learning to tolerate all the sloppy evidence-gathering procedures I was coming to know only too well, all the serious defects in our court system. So I chose to stay where I could be more effective."

Ellen asked anxiously, "Do you suspect Guy?"

Kate observed her concern with regret. "I suspect everyone. Even you."

"*Me*?"

"This scenario. You came in this morning, made coffee. Fergus Parker came into the kitchen, took you back to his office on some pretext, did something offensive, something obscene, something bad enough to cause you to pick up his letter opener... and then you took it from there."

Ellen said furiously, "You can't be serious!"

"Just a scenario to prove a point," Kate said as gently as she could, remembering her usually futile attempts to soothe Anne's temper. "Miss O'Neil, don't be upset."

"You surely can't think—"

"The motivation is a little weak, don't you think?" She was smiling, trying to pacify her, but Kate was amused by her ire; the light brown eyes were narrowed and sparking in anger. "I'd like to be your lawyer if you were arrested on that basis. If what I described actually happened, I see total disgust on your part, I see someone's face being slapped, I see you even resigning from your job. I don't see murder. Why did you try to protect Mr. Adams?"

"I don't see Guy's motivation, either. He disliked Fergus Parker, but everybody did, from what I hear." She hesitated, feeling foolish. "It was pure impulse. He's been very kind to me, I thought I might create an awful problem for him he didn't deserve, make him a suspect."

"When you looked into Mr. Adams' office, was he in there?"

"No! As God is my witness!"

"Was there any evidence of his presence?"

"No. Nothing I can remember."

"Anything on his desk? Papers? A coffee mug?"

She narrowed her eyes in concentration, trying to picture his desk that morning. "No."

"No, there was nothing on the desk, or no you don't remember?"

"No I don't remember," she said, shaking her head. "I was looking out the window at the mountains."

"Are you in love with Mr. Adams?"

"What?" She gaped at Kate Delafield. She stammered, "I— no, I'm—For God's sake, we only just met!"

"His attraction to you is quite evident."

"Really," she said sarcastically, with a vague feeling of offense. She could not reveal to Kate Delafield that she was a lesbian; Kate Delafield's own sexual orientation was not an established fact, and any information furnished might not be subject to confidentiality.

Kate had been carefully watching the range of emotion on Ellen O'Neil's face, assessing the vocal intonations. For now, she decided, Taylor had been correct in his assessment of Ellen O'Neil and her "roommate." She asked sternly, "Since you're so intent on defending him, did it never occur to you that Mr. Adams might be the killer of Fergus Parker?"

"That's *absurd*. He'd have trouble killing a mosquito. He's not the kind to do anything like that."

"How can you make such a judgment when you've only just met?" The spirit and conviction of Ellen O'Neil's responses was consistent and impressive. Yes, she would make an excellent witness.

"I just *know*. From his temperament, the way he *is*."

Soberly, Kate looked at Ellen O'Neil. She had learned that many people—perhaps most—lived decent lives under pressures that kept them on the perilous edges of control; that for many, simply to get through each day with their human decency still intact was the significant triumph of their lives. But for some, the day came when the control crumbled, when they were propelled into acts... "Miss O'Neil," she said with quiet emphasis, "believe me, *anyone* is capable. Some of the most despicable murderers of this century were men who were kind to their children, loved their parents, cherished their wives."

"I suppose you're right," Ellen conceded, unconvinced. "I swear I've told you everything else truthfully."

Kate sighed inaudibly. She knew she could not give anyone else her experience and intuitions. Suddenly weary, she rubbed her face with both hands. "Will you be here the remainder of the day? Home this evening?"

Ellen nodded. "I have to take...somebody to the airport." She added, "But I'll be home after eight."

"There'll be another statement to sign later. And possibly more questions. Thank you for your time, Miss O'Neil."

Ellen rose, moved to the door, turned back. "You're a tough one, Detective Delafield."

Kate smiled. "I take it you don't mean that as a compliment."

"Yes, I do mean it as a compliment."

"Then thank you."

As the conference room door clicked shut, Kate sat in utter stillness, disoriented, drifting in a void. The moment passed; and she sagged in her chair, enervated, profoundly depressed. She struggled against the feeling, shaking her head violently and squaring her shoulders. She had work to do, a lot of work. Reports. Interviews with the other managers and the security guards. Review of the information Taylor had compiled, of the files stacked high on the conference room table. An interview with Mrs. Fergus Parker, who had told her on the phone a few minutes ago in a soft apologetic voice that she had to pick up her children on two different flights at the airport, but would be glad to see Kate at seven o'clock.

Chapter 7

Harley Burton's office was a melange of overcrowded and mismatched furnishings. The desk, huge and oblong, was too large for the room; the chairs too small as if in compensation. Beside the desk were boxes overflowing with books and bookends, plaques, other office paraphernalia. Dozens of photographs crowded the walls and were stacked on the floor, the credenza, the bookcase. A photo in a silver filigree frame dominated the credenza: a woman with whitish hair and cornflower blue eyes stood with arms draped around the shoulders of two teenage boys.

Her hand feeling bruised from Harley Burton's handshake, Kate sat down opposite him and leaned back in the spindly chair, propping her elbows on the metallic armrests. Harley Burton's intense dark stare riveted her to the chair.

"About time you came in. Probably your best suspect, right?" The broad grin uncovered strong but uneven teeth. Like a prizefighter's face, his eyebrows and the bridge of his nose were ridged with bone; a few acne scars pitted his cheeks and chin. Wiry brown hair was clipped short and receded in an even semi-circle from a wide round forehead. His pristine shirt was monogramed in tiny black letters on the pocket, the sleeves rolled up to the elbows of muscular arms covered thickly with brown hair. A large wrist watch of polished stainless steel bristled with gauges and dials. He picked up a huge mug bright with the scene of mounted huntsmen, steam rising from its contents, and took a long draught with evident satisfaction. The rich strong scent of coffee reached Kate.

She asked easily, "Did you want to make a confession, Mr. Burton?"

Harley Burton's laugh came from deep in his broad chest. He was not a tall man, perhaps five-ten, but he projected impressive physical power and energy. "Nope, can't confess. But the man got what he deserved. Helen Parker won't find six pallbearers unless she advertises."

He shook a pack of Carltons vigorously, probed with a finger in the inner recesses and extracted the last cigarette. "Everybody in this damn company smokes mine," he complained with good-natured disgust, crumpling the pack and hurling it into a wastebasket beside the credenza. "Fred's been mooching since Friday, always does when he smokes those stupid little cigars. Gretchen quits every other week, I gave her a pack Monday to keep those begging blue eyes out of my office. Guy's quitting too, he's always in here." He chuckled briefly, drank from his huge mug of coffee.

"For a smoker, you look like a man who takes care of himself."

"Work out on the Nautilus. Play baseball in the summer, semi-pro league. A little basketball, one on one with Gail if I want some real exercise."

"Is Mr. Freeman that good?" Kate took out her notebook.

"Hell yes. The man's a super athlete. He was four, five inches taller, he could've played in the NBA, in my opinion.

Base welterweight champ in the Marines." Harley Burton's eyes surveyed her impersonally. "Terrific shape you're in. Cops, even the women, I hear you have to work out. Calisthenics every day?"

Kate chuckled; she understood that Harley Burton's staccato speech pattern was a symptom of shyness. "Only in the police academy. But we have to pass physical tests twice a year. I swim mostly. And like you, play baseball in summer league." She realized that she liked the man across from her and she asked abruptly, to formalize the conversation, "How long have you worked for Modern Office, Mr. Burton?"

"Harley. Fifteen years, September. Started in the Kansas City plant. Life—all luck and timing, you know. Transfer me anywhere but here, who knows? Might've had Wesley Miller's job by now—he's division head in Philly. Vested in September though, family all taken care of pension-wise. Then I can move on."

"Why do you want to?"

"Long story. You don't understand our business."

"Try me."

"Well, it started months ago, Tampa opened. Sales manager slot. Recommended Pete Webber. Leader, damn fine performer, my top man. Always exceeded his PAF—that's performance against forecast, meaning—"

"I follow. Go on."

He picked up his huge coffee mug again. His cigarette had burned halfway down; he had not taken a puff since lighting it.

"You're quite a coffee hound, Mr. Burton," she observed. "That's the biggest coffee mug I ever saw. Must hold half a pot."

"Just about. Damn inefficient use of time, back and forth to the kitchen a dozen times a day. Anyway, Fergus claimed Pete needed more seasoning, wouldn't pass my recommendation on to Philadelphia. Said he wanted to keep the West Coast team intact till we saw which way the economic climate looked."

Harley Burton sucked breath into his broad chest. "Well, that was acceptable to me. Not agreeable, you understand, just acceptable. But damn hard to sell to Pete Webber, let me tell you. Know the toughest thing I ever do as a manager? Support the stupid decisions of upper management. But I talked Pete into accepting it. Then Fergus changed Pete's account assignments. I don't care what anybody says about sales being nothing but price and delivery, it's a good part personal credibility, customer trust. Some of Pete's accounts he'd been nursemaiding along went to our competitors. And Pete's bonus money went down, his PAF didn't look too good all of a sudden—"

"Did you protest? Argue?"

"Argue? *Argue?* Pounded Fergus's desk to splinters! He said people in Philly orchestrated it, wanted to see how Pete would perform, how he'd react to adversity. You ever hear anything so goddamn *stupid* in all your life? Well Pete reacted all right. Quit. Went to Acme, tried to take our best people with him. They didn't go—loyalty, some of 'em, not all of 'em have Pete's ambition, some of 'em with too much service to quit."

Kate heard a faint cracking sound; her eyes were drawn to Harley Burton's hand which had tightened so powerfully around the handle of his mug that the knuckles and fingers were white.

"Then he demoted me. Said he wanted to shake things up, and I didn't handle my subordinates properly, didn't keep Pete Webber motivated, it was my fault, letting a man like that get away."

Harley Burton, dark eyes narrowed and glittering, stubbed out his cigarette. He fumbled in a drawer for a new pack, ripped off the cellophane and foil, and lit another cigarette, flinging the match; it pinged into the side of a metal ashtray the size of a dinner plate and loaded with ash and cigarette butts of varying lengths. "Sales manager seven years. Seven goddamn years moving from district four—that's Gretchen's job now, the bottom rung—to district one, the corner office. Worked my *ass* off. Even set up an office in my house. Once in a while my wife would come in and introduce herself." Harley Burton's grin was accomplished with obvious effort. "Then Fergus Parker demoted me. And he destroyed it all. All that work, all that commitment, all those years. Men in positions more responsible than mine don't have nearly my ability, I know that. I know what I can do.

But Fergus Parker destroyed any hope I ever had for a career with this company."

Profoundly sympathetic, Kate asked quietly, "Is it unusual, what happened to you? Don't things like that happen all the time in business? Isn't that why they call it a jungle?"

"Detective, that's a damn fine question." Harley Burton emphasized the sincerity of his statement with vigorous nods. "*A damn* fine question. Let me tell you, if it only were a jungle. A jungle's a good place, a fine place to be. That's a pretty good set of rules, survival of the fittest. Good clean competition, may the best man be the leader. The smartest, strongest, the best. But nobody's got a chance against the man who cheats his way to power, who's unpredictable, deceitful, bullies to keep his power."

"Seems self-defeating," Kate said, admiring this man. "It seems a man would soon lose his good strong people, soon damage his own performance."

"Be surprised how long they get away with it. Sometimes they break spirited men, use what's left of their talent. Some people have no guts to begin with. But most people just believe what's told 'em for one hell of a long time. Want to know something about Fergus? He had ability. Didn't need us hating him. He understood how to handle people right. A natural for sales, a hell of a competitor, compete with anybody in this world man to man. Why wasn't that good enough?"

"To be big and strong is never good enough," Kate said, "for a bully."

Harley Burton took a quick puff from his cigarette, tipped up his mug for a final draught. "Hurt all of us," he said quietly, staring at Kate with his piercing dark eyes. "Destroyed Fred's confidence. Tormented Duane within an inch of his life. Duane looks like an idiot, won't rise above where he is but damn good at his job, fine teacher of young people. His people love him. One of his sales meetings, his sales group got up and marched around the table singing their own company version of the USC fight song."

Kate chuckled, and Harley Burton grinned. "That's how well Duane motivates his people. Gretchen..." He frowned, rubbed his craggy face. "Whenever I feel really bitter I remind myself I could've been a woman working for Fergus Parker. Or I could've been Gail Freeman. This region's up in sales, Gail's a big part of it. Good administrative mind, treats his people with dignity, they're damn productive, finest support group I ever worked with. Gail computerized our sales forms and reports, freed up our sales reps from all kinds of paperwork, they just feed in figures now. Figured out a way to get orders into the plant earlier. Our requests for quarterly schedule beat the pants off the other regions. Gail's the best thing ever happened to this office, but Fergus bad-mouthed him all over the company, fought every change, hated every new idea."

"What about Guy Adams? Did he do anything to him?"

"Not that I know of. Guy has his own power sources, Fergus had less control over him than Gail. I think Fergus envied him, maybe hated him for his name, all that class Guy has. I keep telling him he should chuck that PR crap and get into sales. Give me those looks, that charm—hell, I'd drive the competition into the Mojave. I heard Fergus bad-mouth him. I heard him tell *customers* Guy's a fag. From what I see, Guy goes strictly for women—but what the hell, who cares? I mean—what matters? Now Duane, he took Matt Bradford's three kids in for a month when Matt's wife cracked up. I mean, what matters about somebody?"

Kate said, "Police work, you see people from one side only, and always from the negative perspective."

"Some damn good people live in this world. And some of them work right here."

Harley Burton looked at his elaborate wrist watch, began to roll down his shirt sleeves. "Pick this up later? Have to drive to Inglewood, customer visit. Be back at four."

Finishing her notes, Kate nodded.

"Tomorrow all the sales managers are having lunch, pre-funeral celebration. Taking that new girl, what's her name—"

"Ellen O'Neil, I presume you mean."

"Right. Taking her to lunch, Guy's idea. Convince her it's not our habit around here, knocking people off. Like to come?"

Kate said with regret, "It wouldn't really be appropriate. I appreciate it. One last question. What's your assessment of Billie Sullivan?"

"Viper." Harley Burton buttoned his shirt cuffs. "Always wondered if most of the crap Fergus dished out wasn't her idea."

Kate said carefully, "She seems...an unusual personality."

Harley Burton snorted. "Damn kind of you. She offends even Philadelphia people. I figure she had to know something, had some kind of hold on Fergus. What I hear, the women here all hate her guts. Surprised Gail hasn't tossed her out on the street yet."

Kate said mildly, "I've tied his hands somewhat."

Harley Burton pulled a black suit coat from the hanger on the back of his door and shrugged into it and fastened the buttons across his muscular torso. "Well, hurry up and arrest somebody." He yanked open his door. "People here know damn well one of us did it. Everybody in the place is damn nervous, I'll tell you that. Hell, I even threw my own letter opener away."

Kate said, grinning, "I'll do my best."

The objects on Duane Fletcher's curved desk were arranged with mathematical precision: the marble-based pens centered exactly at the outer edge, the jar of jelly beans next to them set slightly in; the stack of typed letters at the exact edge of the royal blue blotter; below the pen set telephone messages in overlapping tiers, apparently in the order they would be returned. To one side of the desk a double-unit bookcase was lined with catalogues identified on their spines by neatly inked tape. Pictures hung along one wall in a straight row and displayed interior designs, one large photograph apparently a project of much pride to the company—Kate remembered seeing it on the wall in Matt Bradford's office. On the credenza was a single photograph, at least ten by thirteen, of a dark-haired, moon-faced woman and two small curly-haired children.

Duane Fletcher hung up his telephone and patted it.

"Greatest invention in the history of the world." He stood, smiling, to shake Kate's hand. "Reach out, reach out and touch someone." His tenor voice contained the treble of pre-puberty.

The inch-wide dark hair ringing Duane Fletcher's bald head extended into thick gray sideburns. His bright dark eyes were set close together, giving him a slightly startled aspect, a comical monkishness; a small mouth was tucked up under a nose that had been surely broken at least once. He wore a purple suit jacket with light blue pinstripes over his bright yellow shirt, the yellow and purple striped tie folded into a wide knot under his short fat neck.

Kate made herself comfortable in one of the two soft leather chairs in front of the desk, and took out her notebook. "What time did you arrive today, Mr. Fletcher?"

Taking a jar of Laura Scudder peanuts from a drawer, Duane Fletcher shook out a handful, offered the jar to Kate. "Call me Duane. Everybody calls me Duane. Always get here at ten to eight. Early bird gets the worm. Just like Avis, I try harder." He tossed several peanuts up and caught them in his mouth.

Amused, Kate waved away the offer of the peanut jar. "You like your job, Mr. Fletcher?"

"So don't call me Duane. The job? Like the saying goes, I've come a long way, baby." His high voice was earnest. "But some days, you know, there've been times ... well, you always figure you could be better off. Put a tiger in your tank, reach for all the gusto you can."

Careful not to smile, Kate asked, "How would you describe your relationship with Fergus Parker?"

Duane Fletcher raised both hands in a gesture of supplication. "How do you spell relief? D-E-A-D. I hate to speak ill of the dead, but plop plop, fizz fizz, oh what a relief it is."

I'm straight man in a comedy act. Kate dropped her voice into stern solemnity. "I understand Fergus Parker made your life very difficult."

Duane Fletcher sighed, a wheezing like an air brake on a door, and ate more peanuts. "He always liked to flick my Bic. But I took a licking and kept on ticking. I tried every way I knew to fly the friendly skies, but the man never spoke a complimentary word. He never threatened to fire me—I must've done a decent job. I guess I had ring around the collar that was stronger than dirt."

Duane Fletcher munched more peanuts. "But I didn't kill him," he said, "if that's what you mean. Not that I didn't want to. I know too well why Helen Parker's stayed drunk all these years, how she suffered with that man. I can imagine how she feels now. We're all well rid of him. We deserve a break today."

"Mr. Fletcher, do you always speak in advertising jingles?"

"*Jingles?*" Duane Fletcher's choirboy voice was incredulous, indignant. "Madam, progress is our most important product. Business had put this country in the driver's seat, made this country snap crackle and *pop*. The best ideas in this country are business ideas. Ford has a better idea—"

Will he ever run out? Kate wondered.

Duane Fletcher gazed at his desk and ran a tidying hand around his fringe of hair. "You really had to take a joke when you were around Fergus. He was really a kidder, you know. Sometimes a little … tough to take." He looked up; his dark brown eyes had the nervous vulnerability of a deer.

Kate asked gently, "Did you ever consider sitting down with him to tell him how much his behavior bothered you?"

"You'd never do that with Fergus. He was always testing you, he'd say it was just a test. Got to thicken that skin my boy, he'd say. Got to be smart and tough or your subordinates'll put their boots in your back."

Kate asked with a smile, "Ever have a subordinate try to put a boot in your back?"

Duane Fletcher's answering smile was shy, boyish. "My subordinates don't even wear boots. And we all love each other."

"Love? Isn't that a little strong? For the business world?"

"Not for my people. They're wonderful, my sales group."

He leaned toward Kate, and even though the office door was closed, lowered his tenor voice to a whisper. "Know the worst thing Fergus ever did to me? I've never been able to tell a soul. Promise you'll keep it a secret?"

Kate said cautiously, "I can't really make a promise like that."

But she closed her notebook and waited. People confessed their most hidden secrets to priests—and to cops. And this was even a more common occurrence for her than for the male cops she knew. People revealed themselves as they never would to their husbands and wives and lovers, their parents, their friends.

"He told me…" Duane Fletcher lowered his voice further, so that Kate had to lean toward him. "He told me…" He swallowed. "He told me he went to bed with Marge. My wife."

He asked in his normal high pitch, "Can you imagine that? Saying that to a man? And that's all he said. Not when or why, he just stared at me with those gray popeyes and said …" He dropped his voice again. " 'Duane my boy, I've been to bed with Marge. And she sure hasn't got much to peddle.'" He wheezed a sigh and looked at Kate with dark button-round eyes that had become moist. "Can you imagine?"

"No, Mr. Fletcher," Kate said softly, "I can't."

"You know, it's kind of different, being called Mister. Maybe people don't do that enough anymore. Here, have some peanuts."

"Maybe all people should have more respect for one another." She accepted the jar and shook several peanuts into her palm.

"I assumed it was just another test, what he said. But I asked Marge. I had to. Just out of the blue I asked her, thinking if it was true I might surprise it out of her. But all she did was get mad as hell and want to come down here and—well, I talked her out of *that*. I mean it would have been my *job*. Detective Delafield?" He fixed his soft misted eyes on Kate. "I'm pretty sure it was another kind of test and he was kidding. Think he was kidding?"

"Yes, Mr. Fletcher," Kate said in her most official voice, summoning all the authority she could muster, "I'm sure he was kidding."

Duane Fletcher reached into his breast pocket, removed a bright purple handkerchief, dabbed at his eyes. "I think so, too."

Kate ate the peanuts. Then she asked, "Did any other employees that you know of—were they given similar...tests?"

Duane Fletcher coughed, cleared his throat. "Well, we all hated him. But poor Gretchen... I heard rumors. But just can't repeat them. I think... I think she got...special treatment. I think he...did some pretty shitty things to her. And Harley, maybe you've heard about Harley Burton?"

Kate noted that Duane Fletcher had moved from the subject of Gretchen Phillips with evident relief. "I understand Harley Burton was demoted," she said.

"Fergus took Harley out of his job and gave it to Fred Grayson for no good reason, just sheer meanness. Harley's a damn hard worker, I was waiting for the day Fergus would move on and Harley'd succeed him, I was *counting* on it. And Fred, once he got that corner office, it was like Fergus had a license to kill him. Pick on me? You should've seen the way he picked on Fred. Called him six ways an idiot in every meeting, even in front of Philadelphia people. And that's career damage, you know. Those Philadelphia people—well, they decide your *career* outside of this office. So I don't know who'll take Fergus's place, what I'll have to put up with now..."

Duane Fletcher gazed mournfully at his empty peanut jar. "I can't believe I ate the whole thing."

Kate smiled, rose. "Anything else comes to mind, Mr. Fletcher, I'll be around." She pulled a card from her notebook. "If there's anything you think of, want to add to what you've said—"

"Right. Nice jacket you got there." Duane Fletcher smiled and touched the fat knot of his tie. "Look sharp, feel sharp, be sharp." He slid Kate's card into his breast pocket.

Kate walked to the door struggling against irresistible temptation. "My card," she said, "don't leave home without it."

Duane Fletcher's high-pitched laughter followed her down the hall.

Gretchen Phillips was on the phone, but she waved Kate in and pantomimed instructions to close the door. She said into the phone, chuckling, "Sure I'll wait, are you kidding? The customer's threatening to throw me out my sixteenth floor window."

Kate sat down, and with increasing pleasure studied Gretchen Phillips, who was drumming almond-shaped coral nails impatiently on the pearl gray cover of an appointment book. Her delicate features were dominated by blue-gray eyes, large and serious, covered by oversize glasses with square bluish frames resting part way down her nose. Glossy black hair framed her face in stark simplicity and elegance. Her lips were finely shaped thinness and lightly lipsticked; in unconscious sensuality she caught her lower lip momentarily in even white teeth. To Kate she was reminiscent of exotic Oriental women with their slight bodies and luminous white skin. The white suit jacket was well-cut gabardine over her filmy lilac blouse, a strand of tiny pearls at the throat.

Her desk was a functional square, and dwarfed by folders, letters, purchase orders, catalogues, notes, messages. The matching credenza was also piled from end to end. The shelves of her bookcase were stuffed with haphazardly arranged catalogues, some splayed open. Strangely, a stapler and staple remover—perhaps vestiges of previous secretarial days, Kate speculated—sat beside two gold Cross pens in a marble base. One painting hung on a wall, a geometric city of striking purples and grays; three other frames leaned against a wall waiting to be hung, their canvas faces turned in. Kate glanced around the chaotic office for a framed photo—all the managers seemed to have one—but there was none. Again she looked at Gretchen Phillips, at her hands: ringless, except for a delicate thin gold band on the ring finger of her left hand, fashioned into a tiny heart.

"Yes, Jerry." Gretchen Phillips sat erect, slender shoulders straight, and picked up a thin black pen with slim fingers. "Wait, wait just a minute." She stood, an immaculately neat anomaly amid the disarray of her office, and took the phone cord to its limit as she pulled a folder out of a pile on the far end of the credenza.

"You're a doll, Jerry," she cooed into the receiver. "What? Hey listen, you got it. Thanks a lot, the customer really appreciates this... Hey, sure. It's a promise. Talk to you soon."

Gretchen Phillips hung up her phone and groaned, sat down and crossed her arms and lowered her head into them and groaned again.

Amused by her dramatics, Kate inquired, "Rough day?"

She lifted her head, removed her glasses, sighed. "Actually, no. Just routine." She extended a hand. "How are you?"

Smiling, Kate took the delicate soft hand, thinking that she was equally lovely with or without her glasses. "Miss Phillips, I won't feel bad at all taking you away from your work for a few minutes."

Gretchen Phillips inclined her head toward the phone. "Jerry Burns. Floor superintendant in Kansas City. If he ever comes to L.A., I'll arrange to be out of town. I've promised him my body and any number of acrobatic sex acts to expedite orders out of that miserable excuse for a factory."

Kate chuckled, and Gretchen Phillips said, "How long did I talk on that call, ten minutes? Twenty, twenty-five calls I handle when I'm in the office, and only one minute of each call with any substance. That's what, three to four hours? Of nothing but bullshit. Know the first thing I do when I get home? Take a shower. Then and only then Chris fixes me a drink."

Kate chuckled again and said sympathetically, "I'm lucky about my work, or at least aspects of it. It seems a lot of people find themselves in jobs they dislike."

"Oh, don't misunderstand, I love it. I really do. I'm very good at my job. I just care too much. I care about the reps who work for me, I really work for my customers. I'm good at finesse work, actually. I think women usually are, don't you?" Kate nodded and smiled. "I'm aggressive and damn thorough. I bet you are too." Again Kate smiled. "And my people, my customers, one thing they know about me, they know I care. They know I work hard and worry about them and *care.*"

"You're an increasing rarity today." She was impressed by Gretchen Phillips. "How long have you been a sales manager?" She knew the answer, but wanted to steer the conversation.

Gretchen Phillips smiled. "Two long, interesting years."

"Is that how long you worked under Fergus Parker?"

The smile faded; her eyes were remote, cold. "Was your choice of words deliberate?"

Surprised, Kate said in a controlled, even tone, "I thought nothing of them one way or the other."

Gretchen Phillips leaned back in her chair, crossed her legs, shook a cigarette from a pack of Carltons and said tiredly, "That wasn't even a test, and I failed. I'm still getting used to not having any more…tests." The word was expelled in a sibilant hiss. "I worked directly for him two years, indirectly for three before that when I reported to Harley Burton."

Kate decided to temporarily deflect her questions into an area that would not invite resistance or animosity. "What time did you arrive this morning, Miss Phillips?"

"Traffic on the Pasadena Freeway was, you should excuse the expression, murder. About a quarter to eight."

"What time do you usually arrive?"

"Seven, seven-thirty. Guess what?" She smiled. "It wasn't me."

Kate returned her smile. "Why not?"

"No motive."

The direction of the conversation was now Gretchen Phillips' choice. "Really? That's not what I hear."

Gretchen Phillips leaned on her elbows and cupped her chin in both hands and looked at Kate with a coyness that seemed self-mocking. "And what is it that you hear?"

"People tell me about Fergus Parker's tests. And that he singled you out for…special treatment."

Gretchen Phillips picked up her cigarette and a thin silver lighter, then tucked the cigarette back into the pack. "No, dammit. Chris wants me to quit and this time I'm really trying to. Guy and I, we're suffering together, helping each other. He's down to three or four a day now. We've decided to keep a pack so we know we've got some, but he keeps the pack half the day, I keep it the other half. We count the cigarettes missing at the end of the day."

"Good idea, reinforcing each other like that."

Gretchen Phillips placed her arms on the desk, leaned forward. Perfume reached Kate, a sweet flowery scent. The eyes looking into hers were a clear and lovely gray-blue.

"Special treatment," Gretchen Phillips said quietly. "I'm glad it's a woman detective asking me about that. Let me try to describe Fergus Parker's special treatment." Her voice was low, calm. "His body was like a big sweaty soft slug. He'd take off his jacket and there would be these huge patches of sweat under his arms. He had a sour smell, like rancid yeast. My God, men can smell like sewers." Her tone was uninflected, her eyes cool, expressionless. "His mouth was big and wet, like one of those fish, what do you call them, groupers? And the cigar smoke on his breath, like burnt feathers. And tasted like varnish."

Kate sat in rapt stillness, compelled by the icy calm, the eloquent ugliness of the words.

"He thought he was wonderfully masculine because he had arms that suffocated me, hands that pawed and hurt. And he'd have his hot perspiration all over me by the time he was finished."

As silence lengthened, Kate cleared her throat. "Miss Phillips, why did you put up with that? I don't see why you had to do that."

Gretchen Phillips smiled.

"You could have complained," Kate said. "Wouldn't quitting have been better?"

Gretchen Phillips swung her chair around so that she sat in profile, looking off toward the horizon of the sun-splashed city below them. She crossed her legs and said in a voice that was dreamlike in its lack of expression, "To want the kind of jobs men have…you surely know how it feels. That hunger for a sense of accomplishment…you surely know about that, too. To have that job you know you would love, know you'd be good at … And then a man tells you he wants you, a man with everything to say about whether you get that job, whether you keep that job. How do you react? How do you handle a man with that kind of power over you, over your life? So many women have even fewer options than I had, they're alone, with children…"

Gretchen Phillips sighed, turned and looked at Kate, hands

clasping the sides of her chair. "Complain? Deana French complained. She was in sales when I was still a service rep. When she first complained she was laughed at because she was overweight and not particularly attractive. Then the men found out she'd actually written a letter to Philadelphia, and Deana just wasn't a good *sport*. After all, she just had to say no, didn't she? What was the big deal? Then the subtleties began. She was ostracized. Given problem accounts, customers who produced more headaches than profit. Her expense accounts were questioned, checked and rechecked. Her performance appraisals—well, Deana quit. But she couldn't leave L.A. because her mother was ill. And draw your own conclusions, she couldn't find another sales job or any other job in our industry. So then she filed a lawsuit. And some men in this office said things under oath in depositions that simply weren't true. And then her mother died and she had a nervous breakdown. She's pulled herself together, the last I heard she was in partnership with another woman in an employment agency."

Kate said, "I had assumed things were better for women in business now."

"For women with stomach, women willing to pay a price. Or with the strength and wherewithal to draw a line. That's what it really comes down to—what are you willing to go through, to accept? Frequently it's easier to quit, give up that job you love, abandon the dreams. But don't feel badly for me. He didn't want me often, and the man didn't really want sex, he wanted the power. He wanted the rumors that he was laying his lady sales manager. His ejaculation was never sex, it was power."

"Miss Phillips," Kate said gently, "there's something I still don't understand. How can you tell me you had no motive for wanting him dead?"

"I may be wrong, and it doesn't matter one way or the other," Gretchen Phillips said, "but I think… I'm pretty sure, you're a lesbian."

Caught totally off-guard, Kate managed to say, "My private life has nothing to do with my work, I don't—"

"I understand. You have no idea how well I understand, it's how I live, too. And you're a police officer, I can't even begin to imagine the pressures on you." She leaned her slender body forward, sending sweet perfume toward Kate once more. "I had no motive because I'm one of the few women who could afford Fergus Parker's price for my job. I met the woman I live with in college. We've been together nine years. Chris and her brother own a small greenhouse, we all live in a little house in Pasadena. She's the reason I won't leave L.A. Chris does wonderful things with plants and...flowers. She touches a plant and it's like a miracle."

The gray-blue eyes were again looking directly into Kate's eyes. "The times with Fergus Parker, I'd go home afterward and bathe and douche and then ask Chris to give me a massage. She loves to massage me. She has big hands, soft and healing. I can't begin to describe how they feel on my body. And when she massages me, there's not a part of me she doesn't stroke and love. And it's like he was never there. As long as there was Chris, Fergus Parker never...mattered."

"This investigation," Kate said. "Your office has been an education."

"I don't think our office is so unusual."

Kate shook her head. "Fergus Parker's replacement will have to be an improvement from your point of view."

Gretchen Phillips shrugged. "At least a different kind of devil. Somebody from another office, I expect. Harley should have the job, but his demotion had to hurt him badly back East. I worked for him when I was a sales rep, he's a terrific guy, a pro, a hard worker who makes all his people want to produce. Duane has no chance. It's the way he handles himself. He's so crazy about his wife you'd think he'd listen to her and have the sense not to wear those gaudy clown suits. Me, I won't be considered. I think this company will be ready for a Martian in higher management before they'll accept a woman. And I don't have enough service anyway. It may very well be Fred." She sighed, donned her big square glasses. "Fred's such an ass. Insecure, afraid to make a decision. It'll be everyone for themselves if he gets the job."

"It would seem Harley Burton has an excellent motive for murder," Kate probed.

"I think the world of Harley Burton. If he did it to Fergus Parker, more power to him. I hope you never prove it."

The phone rang. Gretchen Phillips said irritably, "I told Judy to hold my calls." She picked up the receiver. "Gretchen Phillips." She listened for a few moments, then covered the receiver with a hand. "This is really urgent, it won't take long. I've been working on this customer's problem since—"

"It's all right." Kate rose, took a card from her notebook. "Call me if there's anything you'd like to add."

Gretchen Phillips put her phone on hold. She gave Kate her small delicate hand, then clasped Kate's hand in both hers. As Gretchen Phillips' hands slowly tightened, Kate held the level blue-gray gaze with all the impersonality she could muster. The soft hands finally released her, and Kate walked from the office.

Casting a surveying glance over the ornate furnishings of Guy Adams' office, Kate closed the door behind her. She sat down across from him, and in deliberate silence turned the pages of her notebook, one at a time, to a blank page. *Deep tan* were the first words she wrote. After a moment she added *in February.* No doubt a perfect tan, she thought, probably not even a tan line. A tanned peacock sitting in a bright nest of an office with everything designed to enhance his plummage.

Reminding herself of her obligation to objectivity, she straightened her jacket and looked up at Guy Adams. He was taking a swallow of coffee from a mug of translucent bone china shaped like a loving cup. She examined him more closely. Under the tan, the face was drawn, with an off-color pastiness; under the immaculate tailoring, the shoulders sagged. Pallor could indicate guilt—or shock. Cold judgment told her that when it came to certain of life's realities, Guy Adams was the perfect type to be squeamish, to be lacking in the stomach department. Unlike herself, totally unqualified for garbage collecting. It was comforting irony to think of herself as following in her father's footsteps—in a better paying job, but still cleaning up other people's messes. Her father—dead seven years—had been a sanitation worker in Michigan.

"Mr. Adams, what can you tell me about Fergus Parker's death?"

"I don't—" Guy Adams shook his head and said in a husky whisper, "I'm stunned."

She sighed inaudibly. So much for her best open-ended question. "What time did you arrive this morning?"

"I'm not really sure." Adams' voice was hushed, and he raised it to add, "I had car trouble on the way."

"What kind of trouble?"

"Radiator. My radiator light came on."

"Did you stop at a gas station? Or call an auto club?"

"Neither. It wasn't necessary. I pulled off the freeway and took care of it myself."

Kate made a note, and observed Adams' fretful glance at her notebook. It was not an infrequent reaction. She had always used bound notebooks, believing that her interview subjects were more impressed with the gravity of their statements; and the non-detachable pages impressed juries whenever the notes were entered in evidence.

Deliberately, she made another note, then studied Adams' well-cared-for hands which lay flat on a small, deep green desk blotter edged in gold. "You repaired your own radiator?" She did not soften the sarcasm.

Adams replied with irritation, "I'm perfectly capable of unscrewing a radiator cap. The water level was normal, so obviously the indicator light was malfunctioning." He smiled suddenly, touched fingers to his empty breast pocket. "I can prove it. The radiator cap didn't seem greasy, but I used my handkerchief to wipe my fingers anyway. I tossed it onto the back seat of the car."

Kate made a note in caps. "We'll just pick up the hand-kerchief. Is your car locked?"

"Do you always presuppose people lie to you?"

Kate reappraised the man across from her. Guy Adams was tense and upset, but he had managed a smile; his poise and confidence were inbred and automatic. "It's a good idea in police work, Mr. Adams." She repeated, "Is your car locked?"

"No, no reason to lock it. Nothing in it. It's parked on the first floor of the garage." The smile contained indulgence. "It's a company car," he added.

Meaning you can be careless and not lock it. "Make and license number?"

"Eighty-four Olds Cutlass. Black. One-MEL-something."

"Mr. Adams, try to give me a rough estimate of when you arrived this morning."

"I don't know…There was so much confusion, police cars, police officers…They wouldn't let us up here for a long time …"

Seven-fifty or later, Kate wrote. "I'm sure. How well did you know the victim?"

Guy Adams pondered the question. "Not very well. Didn't want to, you see. I didn't work directly for him and I haven't been in the L.A. office long, only three months. We didn't care much for each other. But—"

"Why not?"

"He's not—he wasn't my kind of person." His finely-shaped mouth pinched downward in distaste. "Crude—very. All the class of a street thug. He treated his subordinates shamefully. Excused his inexcusable behavior by always claiming he was testing people. As far as I know, hardly anyone liked him. I've seen other people like him in offices I've worked in, but no one quite so … so ugly as this man. I did what I could, discussed him with people I know in Philadelphia—but he had a very successful record here. Of course, the people who worked for him made that success, but he got the credit. That's how these things work—"

Guy Adams was now speaking freely, but rambling, and to no useful end. "Yes, I know how it works," she interrupted. "What other company offices have you worked in?"

There was a slight smile. "Quite a number. I started in Philadelphia straight out of college, worked there almost three years. Then they sent me to…let's see, Dallas, Seattle, Chicago—no, Atlanta, then Chicago. Then New York, then out here."

Adams was a relative, Kate remembered—a nephew. "A lot

of transferring. How long have you been with the company?"

"Eight years."

"What exactly is your function?"

Guy Adams sat up straighter and said heartily, "Public relations. Promoting good will with customers. And I work with civic organizations, schools, charities, all that kind of thing. I do lobbying when it's necessary—"

Defensive about his usefulness, she concluded. She prodded, "Why were you sent to so many cities?"

"I carry out assignments given me by the company just like any other employee," Adams said stiffly. "They want me to use my name for the company's benefit, and I use it. They've chosen to spread me around quite a bit."

"That they have," Kate said agreeably. She prodded again, "But still, Adams is such a common name. I don't see why it would be useful except in a company with a name like Adams Furniture."

"My family name is a very great name, to those who *know*." A glint of anger was evident in Adams' green eyes. "My family's English, Guy is an ancient Celtic name, we're descendants of a family branch of Samuel Adams." He paused, his eyebrows raised as if in challenge.

Amused, Kate made an off-hand guess. "The Declaration of Independence."

Adams looked surprised, slightly crestfallen. "Almost everybody thinks of John Adams. Few people know Samuel's name is just above his, the sixth row of signatures. Our family moved from Boston to Philadelphia around the turn of the nineteenth century and started the family business, fine crafted furniture back then." Guy Adams was speaking easily, as if he had related this background many times. "Around nineteen-ten there was a big family squabble and old Guy Adams bought out his two brothers. Unfortunately, my grandfather was one of the brothers who broke away, so I'm not connected to the great Adams fortune. My father was a lawyer. I've had to earn my living just like anyone else."

Only a tiny silver spoon in your mouth, Kate thought acidly. Merely a pedigree that dates back beyond the Revolutionary

War, a job handed to you right after college, travel and a big salary and a car and expense account, enough feeding at the rich end of the Adams trough to indulge a taste for expensive tailoring and these glossy office trappings.

She took her time over her notes. She had always disliked men like Guy Adams, not because their money and position and opportunities were unearned, but because of their assumption that this was the way things should be for them, that advantage and important connections were laws of nature, like leaves growing on trees. There was no knowledge in them—not the slightest conception—of what it was like to have money worries, family worries, to work full time and carry a full load of college classes, to live and work week after month after year on the raw edge of exhaustion. Not for Guy Adams to have parents who suffered guilt at what they could not give, to have a mother who on her deathbed whispered, "Kate, our one dream was to find the money somewhere to send you to college…"

Pen poised over her notes, Kate asked, bitterly anticipating the answer, "Any wartime service, Mr. Adams?"

Guy Adams shook his head. "College deferment. Sometimes I wish I'd gone, even to a war like Vietnam. War, what it does to a man, that's something I'll never experience."

Undoubtedly this perfect man will go into politics some day, she thought with furious disgust, and take his romanticized view of war with him. "Ever been married, Mr. Adams?"

"Briefly. Divorced. One broken engagement. The lady figured I was one of the moneyed Adamses." His smile was self-deprecating. "A lot of people do misread my proximity to the Adams money, my ability to influence decisions made by the company. I work here just like anybody else."

Just exactly like anybody else, she thought, with a brief and poisonous glance around the ornate office. She decided to proceed quickly with her questions before her contempt for this man became obvious. "This morning when you were allowed upstairs, was your office door open?"

Guy Adams' eyes widened, became blank.

"Mr. Adams, it's an easy question." Kate raised her voice, pursued him. "When you came in was your office door open?

Or closed?" She watched acutely as Adams rested an elbow on his desk, rubbed his forehead. He had had the opportunity to compare notes with Ellen O'Neil. Would he lie, as she had lied?

"Gail's always reminding me to close it." His husky voice had dropped to a rasp, seemed distant and tired. "He told me again just yesterday. I can't remember if I did or not. Opening, closing doors, it's so automatic...and when you have things on your mind..."

It was hard to argue with that, Kate conceded as she recorded Adams' answer. But still unlikely he would not remember. "What did you have on your mind that affected your memory?"

"Last night, you mean? When I left? A report I had to finish today ... I was supposed to play racquetball with this guy in my building...I live at the beach now, so I don't have to use the tanning parlors. I swim, play tennis, all that, I play a little golf—"

Kate interrupted the ramble in a pleasant tone. "You're managing to meet people in L.A.?"

"It's a friendly city. Especially the women." He smiled, a tentative, conspiratorial boys-will-be-boys smile.

"Was Fergus Parker a womanizer, Mr. Adams?"

Adams' smile froze. She was gratified that the implied association with Fergus Parker had given such grievous offense. Adams said tightly, "There were rumors. None I care to repeat."

Kate thought of Ellen O'Neil, that she was the kind of warm, enduring woman a Guy Adams would pursue, the kind of woman who possessed resilience and the qualities of character he did not. She felt a gladness about Ellen O'Neil's "roommate," and that she was not attracted to this French poodle of a man. "All right. Whom did you see when you first came into the building this morning?"

Again the green eyes turned blank. Again Adams rubbed his forehead. "Uh, Gail. Fred, I think. Fred Grayson. And the police, of course...I just can't remember. Gretchen and Harley ...but I don't know if they were there already or came later. There was so much confusion, Gail took charge of things and by that time more and more people were arriving—"

"All right. Do you know of any person with a reason for

wanting to harm Fergus Parker?"

"Well, he was disliked, as I said. How deep it went with any individual, I'm not in the best position to say—"

"Or don't want to say?"

"Well, maybe both. Ellen—Ellen O'Neil, she was here when it—when he—hasn't she been helpful?"

"Mr. Adams," Kate said sternly, "I believe Lieutenant Kovich explained the necessity for strict confidentiality in an investigation of this kind. It can only help the killer to know what information or evidence is known about—"

"I haven't discussed it," Adams protested. "I've been with Ellen, we didn't talk about it at *all*."

She rose. "I'll appreciate your continued cooperation." She took a card from her notebook, dropped it on the ornate desk. "Let me know if anything else comes to mind. If I'm not around you can find me or leave a message at the number on the card."

"How long do you think…" Guy Adams trailed off, rubbed a hand again across his forehead.

"We hope to make an arrest soon. I imagine we'll be here several days. Possibly longer."

As she walked to the door she heard the sound of a receiver being picked up, digits being punched. As she opened the door and walked into the hall, she heard Guy Adams: "Ellen? This is Guy. Are you busy?"

Chapter 8

Wearily, Ellen closed her eyes. The day had been eventful enough without this added complication from Guy Adams. "I really can't, Guy. I appreciate—"

Her other line flashed and rang. The button remained lit as Gail Freeman in the next office picked it up.

Guy Adams said, "You might not feel like eating something, that's understandable. God knows, who does? But how about just a drink? We should talk. There's this place—"

"What I really need is to get my mind off what's happened," she said firmly. "I think that's best, and—"

"Ellen ... she suspects me, Ellen. That detective."

"Of course she does, Guy," she soothed. "They have to suspect everybody. Don't be upset."

"Ellen? Change your mind." His husky voice was soft.

"I really can't." She chose her words carefully, depressed and annoyed by the necessity: "It would give me a problem...in my personal life."

He sighed. "I understand. Okay, I'll call you later, check on you. Promise to call if you change your mind? Maybe you'd like to just get out of the building. I could—"

Gail Freeman had appeared in her doorway. In relief she interrupted, "It's dear of you. Sorry, I do have to go." She hung up and said to Gail Freeman, "Poor Guy, he's so upset."

"I know. He's like that. He'll never know how much Fergus Parker hated him—Guy simply can't conceive of people like Fergus Parker." He smiled. "That was our good detective on the other line."

"Did she ask if Matt Bradford's office was open this morning?"

He nodded. "It's always open whether Matt's here or not. The managers need access to those miniature mockups of our office designs, his material samples."

She said wryly, "Detective Delafield has this fetish about closed doors." She stacked several pages together. "I need you to sign last month's overtime report. Philadelphia called this morning—it's a week overdue."

There was no answer; she looked up to see Gail Freeman staring at her, dark eyes lidded in thought. Then he smiled and walked to her, taking a gold Cross pen from the breast pocket of his jacket.

She remembered sitting across from Gail Freeman in his office moments after her introduction to Fergus Parker. "I know I've accepted this job," she had said, "and as much as I'd like to work here, there's no way I could work for that man. I don't see how any woman could. I don't even want to be in the same city."

He had answered in a low firm voice and ticked off points on slender brown fingers tipped with lighter, well-cared for nails. "You'll be working for me, not him. Short of murder, whatever you do is judged by me, not him. His management style offends everyone in the office, it's not restricted to gender or color, and not all of that is necessarily bad. You'll find the dynamics of this place fascinating."

His intelligence and candor had impressed her in the first meeting, and she looked at his ascetic face with reawakened admiration. "Gail ..." She hesitated, unaccustomed to addressing a boss by first name, and groping for tactful words to express her distress at Fergus Parker's disdain for Gail Freeman, a contempt he had not bothered to conceal even in front of Gail Freeman's new assistant. "Gail, he treats you..." Again she hesitated, then selected a word. "...shamefully."

He steepled his graceful fingers. "A few years ago this company was grateful to have a promotable black man to push into a visible position. But now the climate's changed. And I've changed—older, more cautious, more at stake." He smiled, gestured to the family photo on the credenza. "Two years ago I could've walked out, pretty easily duplicated what I have here. But today—maybe not at all. Ellen, years ago I worked in a wheel factory. The memory's just like yesterday. And that takes a lot of the independence out of your attitude, confidence from your step."

He looked at her from thickly fringed, calm dark eyes. "It's Fergus Parker's mean little talent to pick out vulnerability, smell fear like a vampire smells blood. And he hates anything he considers alien." He chuckled, a low, pleasant resonance. "Anything off-white, for example. Please stay, Ellen. I need your help. You won't have a problem with Fergus Parker. Your independence is too obvious. Fergus Parker never plays a hand that's not a sure winner."

"I want to work for you," she had told him. "You're so straightforward, my first honest boss."

"Let's hear it for management," he had said ironically.

Reflecting on this conversation, she watched Gail Freeman read and sign the overtime report. He said, "Our good detective also told me she'd interview Billie Sullivan tomorrow. Know what? I think she just wants to give Billie Sullivan another day on payroll."

Ellen chuckled. "That doesn't quite fit your ogre image of her."

Gail Freeman looked penitent. "I made some flippant remark about her to her partner. I thought he'd pick me up by my tie and slam me against the wall. He told me Kate Delafield was one of the best cops and finest people he'd ever worked with and the citizens of this city should pray for a thousand more just like her. He did explain that she's been recovering from the death of someone close to her. A flaming wreck on the Hollywood Freeway, a really God-awful accident."

Her lover. Ellen knew it instantly. The image of Kate Delafield's strong, suffering face filled her mind. Ellen gazed at her desk. "She's very professional, very good at her job," she murmured. She tried to push away her vision of Kate Delafield's anguish, her unspoken, lonely grief.

Again there was no answer; again she looked up to see Gail Freeman staring at her. Hands in his pockets, he strolled back into his office.

Chapter 9

Stephanie Hale said, "You embarrassed me today."

Ellen, folding underwear into a suitcase, stopped and confronted her, hands on her hips. "*I* embarrassed *you?*"

Stephanie looked at Ellen, ocean-gray eyes cool. "As soon as you called, I came. Didn't I? You were upset enough to call me in the middle of a class, weren't you? I came all that way as fast as I could. Through that rotten Westwood traffic."

"I didn't *ask* you to come. I just needed to *talk* to you. We *love* each other, don't we? But no, super butch has to try and drag her little hot house flower home, her little shrinking violet!"

"Ellen, you found a *dead* man. You could've been killed yourself!"

They were shouting; Ellen lowered her voice and hissed,

"Well, *I wasn't*. And the detective in charge told me I handled myself with great presence of mind."

"So what does she know? When I got there you'd been crying."

Stephanie had taken her jogging shoes from the closet to bring with her, and Ellen picked them up off the bed and hurled them into the suitcase. "For God's sake, you of all people should know tears are *emotion*, not weakness!"

Calmly Stephanie picked up the shoes and slid them into a plastic sack and stacked it neatly on top of her socks. "I had every right to want you out of there, not have you any more upset than you already were."

"Answer me this," Ellen said icily. "If you'd been me, if this had happened in the hallowed halls of UCLA, would you let me take you home because you were upset?"

"There are simply some things I handle better than you."

"What goddamn bullshit."

"So you can swear like a man," Stephanie said contemptuously. "I'm impressed."

"Good," Ellen said. "Fuck you."

She stalked into the living room and sat on the sofa with her arms crossed, furious, as Stepahnie finished packing and walked past her into the kitchen.

Carrying plates of food, Stephanie came into the living room. She deposited the plates on TV trays and sat in her usual armchair, eyes drifting to the television screen as she pushed at the contents of her plate. She lifted a forkful of Stouffer's pasta shells and looked at it. "This stuff," she said.

"You used to love it, raved about the sauce," Ellen said nastily. "Good for jogging, you used to say. Before I decided to go back to work."

"You really want to get into all that again? The food's fine, my taster's off. Okay?"

For some minutes they ate in silence. Grudging the conciliation of changing the subject, Ellen muttered, "I can't stand Dan Rather."

Stephanie contemplated the TV screen, drawing curly strands of graying hair over her forehead with the absentmindedness of habit. Twin furrows formed between her deep set gray eyes. "Honey, what do we do next week when Julie comes and you're not here?"

Ellen sighed inaudibly. "What we did before when I was working. Stephie, why do we have to do anything? She's nineteen. Your kids are both old enough to amuse themselves."

"Ellen honey, we see little enough of them."

Ellen smothered a yawn and tucked her legs up under her, thinking that she was exhausted from this day, and that she saw more than enough of Stephanie's teenage daughters.

Stephanie rose, pulling a gray UCLA sweatshirt down over pale blue jogging pants, and carried their dishes to the kitchen, padding off in her stocking feet, wide shoulders slightly bowed. To the sound of plates being scraped, water running, Ellen punched the remote control impatiently, flipping the TV from channel to channel. She thought: Is it really worth it? Is my heart really into working? Since she hates it so much?

Stephanie came back and sat next to her, thin legs folded under her yoga-style. They sat in silence, watching Richard Dawson joke with contestants on *Family Feud*. Stephanie gestured at the TV. "Turn that idiot off, will you?"

Ellen punched the channel selector. "Right there," Stephanie directed as USC cheerleaders danced across the screen in their maroon-lettered white sweaters and gold skirts, and basketball players shot dozens of basketballs in pregame warmup. "Business is Death Valley," she said. "I don't know what I'd do if I couldn't teach. Be a gardener, maybe." Her eyes were fixed on the screen where players were stripping off their warmup suits.

"I don't feel that way. I wish you'd respect that. What I want to do, I wish you'd take it seriously."

"Baby, I do."

"Last night," Ellen accused, "my first day on the job, you expect a home-cooked meal and a night out on the town."

"Oh for Christ's sake, Ellen. You're not running the damn company. If I can work all day and go out so can you."

Ellen said with dignity, "I had material to read. Technical manuals."

"All in one night?"

"I don't like feeling stupid on a job any more than you would." Anger was swiftly gathering.

Stephanie rose and walked toward the bedroom, pulling her sweatshirt over her head, to change clothes for her flight.

On the way to the airport Ellen rolled down the window, the traffic on the San Diego Freeway drowning out possibility for conversation. They did not speak until they had threaded their way through the airport traffic and pulled up in front of the PSA terminal.

Stephanie set the handbrake on the Fiat. "Ellen darling, it's been too long since we talked. Really talked."

"Months," Ellen conceded sulkily. "For that kind of talking."

"I get back Thursday, Julie comes out next week. Let's talk this weekend. Okay?"

They got out of the car. Stephanie pulled her luggage out of the tiny trunk and then kissed Ellen's forehead, her lips warm and firm. "We have orientation meetings till late tonight. I'll call you tomorrow."

Ellen touched Stephanie's face, suddenly afraid of her leaving, and kissed her cheek, smoothing the fine gray-brown hair back into place behind her ear. She gripped her shoulders.

Stephanie's eyes searched her face gravely. "Ellen? Are you okay?"

She nodded. "Sure." But she was not okay, and did not know what was wrong, nor how to tell her.

She watched Stephanie walk away, garment bag slung over a shoulder; Stephanie looked dignified and distinguished in her herringbone jacket and gray slacks. Stephanie Lewis Hale, Professor of Economics at the University of California at Los Angeles—Ellen was proud of her.

Chapter 10

At five minutes to seven, Kate parked off Colorado Boulevard in Santa Monica, and walked around the corner and down the half block to Fergus Parker's house. She was comfortable in her jacket even this late in a February day, even in usually cool Santa Monica; warm Santa Ana winds had blown in from the desert that afternoon. A large woman in a dark blue muumuu paced the driveway beside the house. Gray roots showed along the part in the neatly combed, curly reddish-brown hair that framed a puffy face.

"Mrs. Fergus Parker?"

Red-rimmed sapphire eyes looked her over, glanced at the shield she had extended along with her ID card, and met Kate's eyes. "Detective Delafield," she said in a soft girlish voice, "I've already answered questions—an officer this morning, and the

Coroner's office a little while ago. My children have just arrived. Do they have to be involved in this?"

"Will we need to question them? I can't think why we would."

"They're very upset, especially my son. Could we possibly talk in the backyard, leave them to unpack?"

"Certainly."

Kate followed her through a latched wooden gate next to the garage, down a path to a tiny yard containing a narrow swimming pool perhaps fifteen feet in length.

"It's a lovely night," Helen Parker said, lowering herself into a deck chair and gathering her voluminous dress around her; rolls of fat settled around her midriff. "The Santa Anas are a lovely and unexpected respite from the winter."

"Indeed," Kate said, sitting across from her and taking out her notebook, thinking that under the circumstances her lyrical praise of the weather fit Gail Freeman's ironic description of the ungrieving Widow Parker, but the red-rimmed eyes did not.

"I don't have much progress to report," Kate said, "or even many questions to ask. We're still putting facts together, gathering evidence which may point to the person responsible. Perhaps we can begin with any persons you know of who were enemies of your husband."

She was taken aback by soft peals of laughter.

Helen Parker said, "His wife. His entire management staff. Most people he came into contact with. Don't be misled by the fact that I've been crying. Those were tears for my children. I *have* them now, and they're never going away from me again."

Kate cleared her throat. "I see."

"No, you really don't. You don't even begin to see." She fished in the pocket of her dress and took out a box of Marlboros with a pack of matches tucked into the cellophane, and lit a cigarette. She glanced at Kate's left hand. "Have you ever been married?"

Warily, Kate shook her head.

"Even so ... you'll understand better than a man would." Helen Parker drew on her cigarette. Her lips were well-shaped, with a trace of lipstick; she held the cigarette gracefully in long plump fingers.

"I haven't had a drink today, Detective Delafield. When Gail told me this morning, I poured myself a stiff one. But then after he left I dumped it into a humidor filled with stinking cigars. I realized I didn't have to drink anymore. Or have to smell stinking cigars in my home anymore. Four hundred thousand in insurance," she said in a musical, contented voice. "The mortgage on the house will be paid, covered by insurance. Stocks and other assets I've yet to find out about. No will, of course. Fergus never thought he would ever die. It's all mine and the children's, as soon as this is over and his body's been disposed of. It's been a difficult choice between letting the worms go at him, or reducing him to ashes. But it's still so hard to believe he's dead I think I'll feel better with the ashes."

Kate cleared her throat again and closed her notebook to concentrate on this remarkable woman. "Feeling as you do, why did you stay married to him?"

The jewel-like eyes glittered. "As you've already surmised, Mrs. Parker drinks a little. Nine years ago the first time, then four years after that he put me in one of those places they advertise on television. Of course I came home and took one look at him and started all over again. But the point is, it's documented. I did leave him once, you see, and took the children. He went crazy. Somebody actually did something to *him*. My lawyer convinced me that I'd never win a custody battle, not with my drinking history, and Fergus swore he'd get witnesses to say I'd done everything from molesting children to masturbating in public."

She drew deeply from her cigarette. "I wish I could get you something to drink."

"I'm fine, thank you. I appreciate it."

"Anyway, when I came back after trying to leave, Fergus made new conditions for our marriage. In exchange for being allowed to keep my own children, all I had to do was cook and clean and perform other ... services on demand, certain ... practices which I had always before refused to do. And Fergus's appetites were far more gross than anyone could ever imagine."

A light ocean breeze disturbed Kate's hair and rustled the folds of Helen Parker's dress. Helen Parker raised her face to the wind, closed her eyes, inhaled deeply, and smiled. "When this is over," she said quietly, "I'm going to treat myself to a very expensive month at a place called *The Golden Door*. It's a spa in Escondido where they perform miracles with diet and exercise to get you back in shape. I'm only forty-four. I used to be an attractive woman. I intend to be again."

Dreamily, she smoked her cigarette, gazing into a distance beyond the swimming pool. Kate remained silent. Cigarette smoke carried to her on the wind. It had been twelve years since she smoked, and she still sometimes missed it.

"Your children," she said finally. "What was their relationship to their father?"

"Fergus loved them. His children and his parents and his two brothers, they were flesh of his flesh, and they saw a side of Fergus none of the rest of us ever did."

Kate was unable to resist asking, "Why did you marry him?"

Helen Parker dropped the cigarette into the grass. "If there's a reason, I've blanked it out of my mind. I refuse to acknowledge any good I might have once seen."

Kate remained silent again, and Helen Parker smiled. "Aren't you going to ask my whereabouts before eight o'clock this morning? I'd be disappointed if you didn't."

Kate smiled and opened her notebook. "Why don't you tell me."

She gestured vaguely. "I was with Rita Jensen next door fixing pancakes for her kids. I do that sometimes if I'm up early."

"Mr. Parker arrived at the Becker Building at six-fifty-three. Did he often leave the house so early?"

"Unfortunately, no."

"Do you know why he went in early this morning?"

"Not specifically. He mentioned a phone call from the East he had to take before the office opened. He seemed unusually cheerful."

Kate touched her pen to her chin, thinking. Gail Freeman

could contact the appropriate people in Philadelphia to check calls from there to Fergus Parker. She made a note, then asked, "What did he have for breakfast?"

"A light snack of ham, sausage, three eggs, three slices of toast, orange juice, and two Cokes."

Kate smiled as she busily wrote. "Coffee?"

"Never drank coffee. He was a Coca-Cola addict. Drank gallons of it. Beginning first thing in the morning. Belched gas from both ends day and night."

The mention of Coca-Cola reminded Kate of the over-turned bar in Fergus Parker's office. "What were his drinking habits?"

"He'd have a little rum in his Coke at night, but not much. Drink a little red wine if he was really celebrating something, like cheating a customer."

"What about the people at Modern Office? Did you see them much? Did you entertain frequently?"

"Not frequently. Fergus preferred to have one or two over occasionally. He loved to make the ones who weren't invited nervous and suspicious. Once a year there was a command performance, all his staff. Fancy, catered, everybody eating tiny canapés, edgy and worried about saying something he'd jump on and ridicule all night."

"Did you notice animosity from any employee that seemed especially intense?"

She sighed. "That's so hard to say. Like measuring inches of evil. I know he did something despicable to Harley Burton. Harley's a fine man, a good person. I think poor Duane suffered the most. Duane's one of those roly-poly foolish little bald men you sort of automatically tease anyway, but Fergus used a cleaver, not a needle."

"Mrs. Parker—"

"Helen."

She decided that this one time she would violate her rule about first names. "Helen, I'd like to at least walk through your home, it would take perhaps five minutes. To gain a better picture of the various facets of your husband's life. Perhaps I could be…a tax assessor?"

"You're very kind, Detective Delafield."

She let Kate in the back door, into a roomy and well-equipped yellow kitchen aromatic with cooking food. Kate realized she was hungry. Fergus Parker's house was split-level, three bedrooms and a family room, and in a disarray that aroused in Kate memories of several pain-blurred days in her own house. In the living room, cardboard boxes were half-filled with books and plaques. Desk accessories, golf trophies, photographs were strewn across an overstuffed velvet sofa and loveseat. A big square desk stood bare, pushed against a wall which had been stripped of its pictures; Kate could see the lighter squares in the paint. In one of the bedrooms, a plump young girl with reddish-brown hair unpacked a suitcase; her dark-haired younger brother, his eyes the color of Helen Parker's, lolled on the bed.

"Tax assessor," Helen Parker said as the young people looked at Kate.

The boy scowled. "You picked a fine time."

The girl said, "Aren't you working a little late?"

Kate said, "You know how inefficient the government is."

There were chuckles, and Kate walked on, to the master bedroom.

The bed was stripped down to the mattress, the room was a chaos of boxes filled with men's clothing and toiletries.

Helen Parker said in a thick voice, "I don't know if I can live here anymore."

"Helen, it's a nice house. A good area to bring up kids." Kate spoke in a low firm tone. "Get a new bed, new bedroom set if you want, paint the place. It's a real nice house for a family."

Helen Parker nodded. "You could be right."

"Give it some time."

At the front door Kate said, "I'll call if I have any more questions. We'll bother you as little as possible."

Without a word, Helen Parker extended her hand. Kate held the big soft hand moments longer than necessary and looked into the beautiful sapphire eyes. "Helen," she said, "I hope your children will always be good to you."

Chapter 11

Kate drove off for dinner.

She had never realized until the past few months the difficulties, the dispiriting awkwardness of dining alone in a good restaurant. Because of her profession she had had to be cautious, circumspect in her personal life, but there were a few close friends who had been fully supportive; there had been no lack of offers of companionship. But she had discovered that she was less and less able to be with women who brought back memories of Anne and herself together, and the recent months had been a time of gradually increasing isolation.

Patiently, she drove around Santa Monica searching for a place lacking formality but not a coffee shop or cafe, and finally stopped on the edge of Venice near the beach. Sea Spray lacked a liquor license but had bright curtains and hanging plants and white tablecloths. She settled herself gratefully in a small leather booth.

She liked Santa Monica, always had; but Anne had disliked the misty moodiness of oceanside towns. The rent control controversy had quieted somewhat, and maybe she should try to move here now, rent an apartment. Sell, get out of Glendale regardless of the uncertain Southern California housing market. Unlike Helen Parker, what did she want now with two bedrooms and a convertible den and two baths and three orange trees in the backyard? An excellent investment, the real estate agent had congratulated them eight years ago. A real home and a good neighborhood, Anne had exulted, brown eyes glowing...

She had not clung to other mementoes. Anne's clothing, her jewelry, had gone immediately to her sister in Santa Barbara. Snapshots and other recorded memories of their lives had been packed in boxes, placed in storage. She had packed away certain dishes and books, odds and ends that had transfixed her with the agony of memory, until the day came when she could bear to look at everything again. Only Barney was still there, the collie they both had loved, who had protected Anne all the evenings and nights Kate was called away to protect and to serve others ... Why should she continue to hold onto the house she was so unwilling to return to each night?

She opened her menu. Preferring a double scotch, she settled with little regret for half a carafe of wine. She read her notes of the Fergus Parker case and evaluated the newest pieces of the mosaic as she selected the crispest pieces of lettuce from her salad.

She had taken the file photos of Modern Office employees downstairs to the garage. The attendant, she had quickly discovered, could just as well have stayed home and collected his paycheck for all the care and attention he gave to his job. Every face in the photographs was familiar to him; he could not remember seeing anyone in particular that morning, had not seen anyone running in the garage. Nothing unusual at all—except for someone coughing.

"Man or woman?" she had asked.

"Man."

"Where in the garage was it coming from?"

"I dunno, behind me somewhere."

"Why did you notice?"

"Coughing his lungs out."

"Why didn't you investigate?"

"What the hell do I care about somebody coughing? Besides, cops were pulling in, they could do their own damn investigating."

Taylor's analysis of the guards' ledger had not revealed any unusual pattern to off-hours activity at Modern Office. Fergus Parker had made no previous early morning visits this year, only four last year. Each of the managers had come in early from time to time, none recently.

At her request, the two guards had recreated their actions after Ellen O'Neil's phone call. Rick Carlson had been on duty; Mike Sutherland had finished his final inspection and was in the guard station. When Ellen O'Neil's call came, Carlson called the police, shouting for Sutherland who came out of the guard office, heard Carlson on the phone with the police, and immediately secured all four elevators, placing them out of service. Sutherland ran to the staircase and released the hydraulic mechanism that lowered the mesh gate on the garage level. Sutherland then refused to wait for the police, insisted that they go up together to check on the safety of Ellen O'Neil. The guards' estimate of how long it had taken to fully close off the upper floors of the building after receiving the call from Ellen O'Neil: forty-five seconds to a minute, no more.

Using a stopwatch, Kate and Taylor had experimented, Taylor's face comically unhappy at having to hurtle his two hundred and twenty pounds down sixteen flights of stairs. They took turns, Kate first; but she had stopped abruptly on the fifteenth floor and called for Taylor. Rolled up against a wall was a Carlton cigarette butt which had burned almost to the filter, a three-quarter length of ash. On the pale green wall was a small black smear: the cigarette had been flung, not merely discarded. Taylor collected the cigarette and ash in separate envelopes, and Kate began her run again. She made the garage in a minute and fifty-two seconds; Taylor's time was two minutes, eight seconds. At Kate's insistence they made the run one more time. Her time was a minute-fifty; Taylor, two minutes-fifteen.

The cleaning personnel, who arrived at five o'clock, had provided two pieces of information. The stairway was swabbed twice a week, Tuesdays and Fridays. And the portable bar in Fergus Parker's office had been in its usual position away from the desk when the office was cleaned Monday night.

Kate's veal chop arrrived; she put her notes away.

Ellen worked her way through the airport traffic and back out onto Century Boulevard, thinking about the weekend Stephanie had proposed. They had had eight such weekends in their two years together—spiritual housecleanings, Stephanie had called them. Naked in bed, eating delicatessen food, smoking joints, drinking wine, exploring each other's bodies and psyches, a weekend of loving, sleeping, talking. Hour after hour, warmed in the concentrated glow of Stephanie's attention... Why was she not as eager as she had always been before?

Troubled, depressed, she parked and walked through the underground garage, cautiously watching the shadows as she always did since the rapist had come from behind a parked car a month ago and seized a woman who lived on the top floor.

The raspy voice of Bob Seger seeped into the upstairs hallway; the erratic guitar rhythms of *Night Moves* seemed aggressive, ominous. Her apartment was inky black, seemed possessed of a sinister silence. She walked quickly through the rooms turning on all the lights. She switched on the TV, searched through the stack of economics periodicals in the rack beside the sofa for the latest *Time*. But she stared at the curtain billowing over the slightly open balcony door, alert and uneasy.

Kate ate her meal with enjoyment, and continued to contemplate the pieces of evidence in the Fergus Parker case.

So many aspects were puzzling. Why had Fergus Parker arrived early? Why had he—or someone else—pushed the portable bar close to his desk at seven o'clock in the morning? Most inexplicable of all, why was there no sign of struggle? Fergus Parker must have known well the specific enmity each individual in the company felt for him. How could a killer catch him so off-guard that he did not—or could not—defend himself?

And another problem—the killer was a coffee drinker, had finished nearly half a pot, according to Ellen O'Neil. Wouldn't he or she bring coffee to Fergus Parker's office? How could the killer run down sixteen flights with a container of coffee in hand? There were no signs of spilled liquid anywhere on the upper stairs—she had checked on hands and knees. Possibly the killer had carried an empty container. But that bespoke too much coolness. Amateur City, Taylor had called this homicide, and experience told her that premeditated or not, after the crime this amateur killer had reacted without thought to what circumstances had dictated.

Ellen O'Neil had responded instantly to sounds of flight and Fergus Parker's death throes—but how long had she delayed in calling the guards? That was the other essential element to be added to the mosaic. If she had acted swiftly, the killer would have had precious few seconds to get down and out of the building before every escape route was cut off.

Kate finished her coffee, reflecting. Except for Luther Garrett, the outside sales group, and a computer operator who had been out since Friday with the flu, she had met or seen all current employees. Depending on the timing of Ellen O'Neil's actions, she could at least place the killer's physical condition within certain parameters.

She glanced at her watch, decided to call Ellen O'Neil.

Her scrupulous inner voice whispered, you don't need to. You can wait until tomorrow. You just want to call her because she is like Anne and you want to hear her voice...

Someone came down the hall; footsteps paused outside Ellen's apartment; something brushed against the door. For some moments she sat frozen; then she tiptoed to the door and peered through the peephole. There was no one visible. Chilled and frightened, she checked the lock, the security chain.

She leaped as the phone shrilled.

"Miss O'Neil? This is Detective Delafield."

"Oh. Yes, how are you?" She was absurdly happy to hear the calm, authoritative voice.

"I have a few questions about the timing of some events this morning. Am I disturbing you? The questions could wait till tomorrow."

"No, really, I'm—no, you're not disturbing me at all." Her own voice seemed high-pitched, foreign.

"Miss O'Neil, are you all right? You sound—"

"To tell you the truth—" She broke off, remembering the sarcastic response the last time she had used that phrase. "I'm alone tonight, I feel very nervous. I don't know why. I've been alone many times before and it's never bothered me, but I thought I heard someone just now..."

"It would be very strange if you weren't strongly affected by what happened today. But isn't there someone—" Kate cleared her throat. "Don't you...usually have someone there with you?"

Ellen called herself a fool. Of course this detective in charge of a major investigation would know about Stephanie. Detective Taylor—any of the police officers on the scene—would have passed along the information that Stephanie had come this morning to be with her. Ellen said, "She left tonight for an economics seminar in Berkeley."

"I see. Let me suggest this. Perhaps I can make you feel more assured about your safety. I'm in the area, I'll be glad to come over and check things out where you live. Or perhaps you should call a friend, stay with someone tonight."

"Would you come over?" she asked very softly. "I'd be very grateful." She was not about to call Marcie and Janice. Stephanie would find out and she'd never hear the end of it, especially after what they had quarreled about tonight. "I can answer your questions, give you something to drink. Would that be all right?"

Kate Delafield was no more than five minutes away; Ellen gave her directions.

Chapter 12

The apartment building was fronted by a date tree on a postage-stamp lawn divided by a sidewalk. Four evergreens clung to the building, sparse ivy climbed over the roof. From the mail slots Kate saw that Ellen O'Neil lived on the first floor, which was elevated above ground by a subterranean parking level. She surveyed both sides of the structure, frowning at the presence of balconies, then buzzed the apartment.

Ellen answered her knock immediately, smiling. "Hi. Thanks for coming."

To Kate she looked younger and even more feminine in jeans and a man-tailored shirt—much like Anne used to look; but Anne had liked khaki pants, the kind with back pockets that buttoned. "No trouble at all," she said. "Miss O'Neil, you should always ask who it is before you buzz someone into this building. And use your peephole every time, even when you expect someone."

Ellen was momentarily irked. "You're right, I suppose. You know what you're talking about. I just hate living that way…"

"Understandably." Kate examined the door lock. "It's not the way I grew up, either. I come from a small town in Michigan. This lock," she said. "Sturdy but not deep enough into the frame. Tell your apartment manager LAPD says you need a dead bolt half an inch in." She took a card from her notebook. "Give them this. Tell them also the garage needs higher wattage."

"Thank you." She watched, smiling, as Kate went over to the balcony. She felt at ease and secure with this woman.

Kate frowned at the balcony door and the transparent curtain over it, a slow billowing in the night air. She pushed the curtain aside. Several plants were visible on the balcony, a small wooden table and two light aluminum chairs. A broom handle leaned against a wall on the inside track of the door.

"The brace is a good idea," Kate told her. "Be sure you always use it, don't get careless. One case I saw …" She decided not to describe the apartment just off Pico and the body of a young woman in a room awash with blood. "Even though you're a good fifteen feet above ground level, you should consider keeping the balcony door closed and locked when you're in here alone at night. This curtain—with lights on, you can see right into the room."

"Feel free to close it now," Ellen said. The room had become chill with the night air.

Kate did so, and moved to the window. "Get some locking devices at a hardware store, Miss O'Neil. They're easy to use, fit right over the runners. A few more safeguards will make you feel that much more secure." As secure as anyone could feel in this city… And assuming someone didn't really want to get in here, didn't use glass cutters or a suction cup.

"Thank you. I'll do everything you say. What can I get you? We have beer, fruit juice, coffee…" She shrugged apologetically. "Stephanie won't allow liquor or soft drinks in the house." The righteous Stephanie also kept a stash of marijuana in the den, but she couldn't very well offer that to a detective from LAPD.

"Any of those is fine. I'll have what you're having."

Ellen said with a grin, "I'm not having any of those. I like a cup of hot chocolate at night."

Kate's throat closed. She swallowed and managed to say, "Fine. I'd like that. I haven't had hot chocolate for...months."

I've struck a memory again, Ellen thought helplessly, moved by the pain she had heard in Kate Delafield's voice. But I don't know how not to. How very much she must have loved her.

Reluctant to leave, Ellen said, "Why don't we take care of business first? What did you want to ask?"

Kate sat on the sofa next to Ellen and leafed through her notes, gathering her thoughts. She was suddenly bone-tired; her throat still ached with the anguish of memory, there was a stinging under her eyelids. Emotion had been ambushing her all day, seemed perilously close to the surface again. And she was exhausted. The wine, she thought, I should never drink when I'm working.

She cleared her throat. "It's possible the killer didn't have much time to exit the building. How long would you say it took you to go from the hallway to the lobby after you saw the body?"

Ellen touched her fingers to her temples, concentrating, reliving the moments. "Fifteen to twenty seconds," she said finally.

Kate nodded. Better than she had hoped. "How long did it take to find the number and call the guards?"

"I found the number right away, but I didn't call right away. I was too scared. Of being seen, heard. Another fifteen seconds ... Maybe twenty."

"How long did it take Carlson to answer?"

"He picked up the phone before it finished a ring."

"And the conversation?"

"Brief. He had trouble hearing me, I was whispering. But it was brief. Fifteen seconds at the outside."

Kate sat tapping her pen against her chin. Now that the detective was preoccupied, Ellen murmured, "Excuse me," and rose to fix their hot chocolate.

"Sure," Kate said absently, adding numbers on a blank page

of her notebook. Using Ellen O'Neil's figures, it had taken a total of forty-five seconds to complete the call to Rick Carlson, another minute at the outside for Carlson and Sutherland to close off the building—allow another ten to fifteen seconds error factor. A minute fifty-two it had taken her, Kate Delafield, to get down those steps in reckless flight. The killer had exited from the staircase with scant seconds to spare before the gate had come down. The killer therefore had to be above average in physical condition. Kate leaned back and reviewed her physical impressions of the employees of Modern Office, Incorporated.

In the kitchen, Ellen scalded the milk, spooned and stirred mix until the chocolate was thick and perfect; she poured it into two mugs, arranged a plate of shortbread biscuits, and carried a tray into the living room. And stopped, staring at Kate Delafield.

Kate had looked up at the sound of footsteps. The face was indistinct in shadows, but framed in the light of the kitchen doorway was the small lithe body, the soft wavy hair. And she held the tray of hot chocolate just as she had for so many nights of Kate's life.

"Anne," she breathed.

Carefully, Ellen set the tray on the coffee table. Kate Delafield had dropped her head into her hands. In the anguish of her understanding Ellen reached blindly, gripped shoulders, squeezed them hard with her fingers. Kate Delafield raised her face, a waxen mask of suffering, her light blue eyes glittering with tears.

"I look like her," Ellen said. "Like Anne. Your lover."

Kate closed her eyes in her struggle, but the supports gave way, beginning deep in her stomach, and as Ellen sat down and took her into her arms, her entire body trembled, then shook violently. "Oh God," she choked.

Ellen whispered, "Have you never cried for her?"

The head pressed into the side of her neck shook no.

"You need to. You need to cry for her." She lay back and drew Kate to her.

Ellen held her, rocked her, clasped the shuddering body

close against hers. "It's okay," she murmured again and again, "it's okay. Cry, it's okay."

The pain was in layers. She cried through the pure agony, then reached the images, and the words were forced from her: "Burned, burned, parts of her melted, charred ... she didn't have a chance...the tanker fell on the hood, she couldn't get out...the metal was all fused, she burned, she burned..."

Ellen unbuttoned her shirt, gave her her bare breasts; they were quickly wet with hot tears.

For a long time after the tears stopped Kate took deep wracking breaths, her face buried in the deep soft warmth of Ellen's breasts; Ellen's hands were in her hair, holding Kate's face to her. Then Kate's hands took Ellen's hands away and she sat up, her eyes red, her face splotchy. Her eyes met Ellen's, glanced away.

"Here." Ellen reached to her, held Kate's head with one hand on the back of her neck, dried her face with her shirt. Kate took the shirt, gently wiped the wet breasts.

Ellen said, "Do you have a handkerchief?"

Kate nodded, reached into a jacket pocket.

"You need to blow your nose," Ellen said. "You're terrible at crying. You don't know how to do it at all."

Kate managed a smile. To allow her some moments of privacy, Ellen picked up the mugs and took them to the kitchen. She poured the chocolate back into the saucepan to reheat, went back through the living room and into the bedroom. Kate was sitting with her head bowed; she turned slightly when she heard Ellen, but did not look up.

Ellen pulled on a sweatshirt, returned to the kitchen. She served their hot chocolate again. Kate's eyes were still reddened but her skin coloring had returned to normal.

Ellen sat beside her. "When did she die?"

"Five months ago. You do resemble her."

"I feel honored to look like someone who was loved so very much."

Tears sprang again to Kate's eyes but she sipped her chocolate, her hands steady. "How did you know?"

"About Anne?"

With effort, Kate smiled. "Among other things."

"Gail—my boss said that Detective Taylor mentioned you'd lost someone close to you not very long ago. I—I just knew. Somehow I just did."

"Do I have an L on my forehead? What made you think I'm a...lesbian?" She could not prevent the slight hesitation; reticence and caution had become ingrown—self-protective behavior on which her professional survival depended.

"I guessed when we first met. I can sometimes tell. I think I tend to see it in women—" Seeing she was trapped, she admitted, "—that I find attractive."

Kate smiled again. "Thank you. After twelve years with one person you wonder if you're still attractive to anyone else."

Ellen sipped her chocolate, awkward and uncomfortable with what she had confessed, even though she knew that by physical definition at least, she herself was attractive to Kate Delafield.

Kate said, "I haven't cried since I was small... You must be clairvoyant, knowing that as well."

"I lost my father a little over two years ago. He was an enormous presence in my life, we were very very close. Now I know I was in deep shock. I went through his funeral but I don't remember much—"

"Anne's was like a dream."

"One night a full four months later I realized my father was dead. And I just fell apart. I cried and cried. For hours. I think when a person means that much the only way you can live through it at first is to have your mind blank it out. Like an anaesthetic during an operation. But then the anaesthetic wears off—"

"Yes," Kate said. "I'm sorry."

"Don't do that." Ellen's voice was firm, quiet. "I think it would be good if you stayed here tonight."

There had been nothing even faintly sexual in the invitation. Kate looked at her unbelievingly.

Ellen said, "I understand what you're feeling right now about Anne. And you understand my anxieties. Both of us should be with someone tonight—tonight we have mutual needs. You said

I should stay with a friend. I feel very safe with you. I don't think you're dangerous, Detective Delafield. Am I wrong?"

Kate said tiredly, "You're not wrong. I don't have a halo. No cop does. But no, you're not wrong."

Ellen's voice softened. "Tomorrow I'll go back to being me, you go back to being a tough cop. Deal?"

"Deal," she said, resisting the impulse to apologize again. "But I did come here tonight to see that you're safe. I give you my word on that—you'll be safe in every way."

"Thank you." She realized that dealing with a sexual advance from Kate Delafield was a possibility that had not occurred to her. "One thing we do need to get settled first—I refuse to spend the night with a woman I have to call Detective Delafield."

It was the first time she had heard Kate laugh, and she grinned, liking the warmth of the sound.

"You're right, Ellen."

"Make yourself comfortable, Kate. I'll get a few things ready in the bathroom."

Thinking of the waxen suffering on Kate Delafield's face, she laid out a towel and a disposable toothbrush, took a pair of Stephanie's pajamas from a drawer. Would it be worse to lose a lover than a parent? She caught herself—told herself guiltily that of course she would go to pieces if anything happened to Stephanie; it was simply too difficult to conceive of such a thing.

She came back to find Kate watching television. She had taken off her jacket; the sleeves of her simple white blouse were rolled to the elbow. The jacket was neatly folded over the back of an armchair, but a thin leather strap was visible, part of the holster apparatus of her gun, Ellen realized; Kate had tucked the weapon under the jacket to be out of sight. Kate looked drawn and exhausted; but she sat erect, body tilted slightly forward as she gazed at the television screen.

She had always liked the alert features of intelligent women, but she wondered if many other women would find Kate Delafield as attractive as she did. The tight polished planes of her face would be too hard for some; even her mouth, which was full, was set in a firm straight line; and her eyes were that cool color of blue…But there was one endearing element of physical vulnerability: the graying hair was so fine that it had the unruly shapelessness of a child's hair.

She sat beside Kate, smothering a yawn as she tried to discern what she was watching—PBS, something about evolution. They were both being polite, she realized. "Look," she said, "I know it's only a little after nine, but it's been a long bad day for both of us."

Kate picked up the remote control, extinguished the picture.

"Bathroom's all yours, Kate."

Hearing the shower run, Ellen remembered her father again, the night she had spent alone crying for him. Kate came out of the bathroom; Ellen motioned with her head toward the bedroom and brushed past her into the bathroom.

Kate contemplated the king-sized bed, decided the side with the digital clock radio on the nightstand was probably Ellen's. She turned down the heavy satin spread. Her guess was confirmed by two economics texts on the other nightstand, the box of man-sized Kleenex behind the lamp. She lay in bed cool and relaxed, strands of her hair pleasantly damp from the shower, Listerine still strong in her mouth, and wondered about the woman Ellen O'Neil lived with. A professor of economics at UCLA, Taylor had told her—who had been mad as hell when Ellen refused to leave with her. The pajamas were long enough but too snug; their owner was as tall, but more slender than she. The owner's first name was Stephanie—and that was all she knew about her.

Exhausted from her spent emotion, warm and drowsy, she watched Ellen come in wearing a thigh-length rose nightshirt; she turned out the light and got in beside Kate, smelling of soap and a sweet and pleasant scent that was not perfume—body lotion or face cream, Kate sleepily decided.

Ellen's hand grasped hers. "Good night, Kate."

Kate turned on her side toward her. "Good night, Ellen."

Her hand still clasped in Ellen's, she plunged into sleep as if bludgeoned.

Ellen was awakened by the blanket being pulled off. The clock digits glowed 12:05. Kate lay rigid beside her, breathing in gasps, tangled in the sheet and blanket, arms and legs twitching.

"Kate," she murmured, rising on an elbow, leaning toward her, knowing not to touch her. "Kate, wake up."

Released from a dream of freezing, of clawing at a transparent glass cage, Kate jerked awake and sat up, her body tense and chilled.

In the street light from the window Ellen saw the pallor of Kate's skin, the faint sheen. She sat up, brushed fingertips over the light film of perspiration on Kate's forehead. She touched an arm and felt gooseflesh through the thin cotton pajamas. Kate shivered, and Ellen took her into her arms and drew her down, pulled the blanket over them, slid her hands under the pajama top and smoothed the cold pimpled flesh with her palms.

Increasingly aware of the soft contours of Ellen's body under hers, the clean scent of the silky hair against her cheek, Kate relaxed under the warm hands soothing coldness and tension from her.

The planes of Kate's back were firmly muscled, her body full and solid—much different from Stephanie's. Curious, Ellen curved her hands around her ribs, and as Kate raised herself slightly in a welcoming of her touch, she explored the softness of her stomach, flatter, tighter than Stephanie's despite all Stephanie's jogging. She slid her hands up to Kate's shoulders and gripped them, enjoying the breadth and fleshiness of them, their unmistakable strength.

Kate watched her. Ellen's eyes had been closed as her hands moved, but now as she grasped Kate's shoulders, her eyes were wide and dark in the dimness of the room. Her body warming with desire, Kate cupped the delicate face, strands of curling hair thick around her fingers. Her fingertips caressed a silken throat. Ellen's eyes closed.

Kate took her hands away. Regardless of who had initiated this, it had already gone too far. She had given her word.

Ellen gazed into the shadowed face poised gravely above hers. She moved a hand over Kate's forehead and into fine hair feathery in her fingers. Images of Kate came to her—the steeliness of her during this day. All thought narrowed into a single focus: to feel that strength. Her arms encircled the broad shoulders. "I'm not glass," she murmured, "I won't break."

In the tightening embrace of Ellen's arms Kate kissed the silken throat, and her hands found the silkiness under the nightshirt. Soon Kate slid the nightshirt off, impatiently stripped off her own pajamas. To a soft sound in Ellen's throat, she took Ellen fully into her arms.

She was supple and delicate like Anne, but nothing like Anne. Yielding and responsive in these first moments when Anne would have been tigerish and aggressive. Ellen's gentle yielding was utterly different, her lips melting sweetness, her soft arms warm, and trusting. Hunger rose, distinct in its shape: to give more and more pleasure, to feel every response from the tender woman in her arms. Her lips left Ellen's; desire sharpened as Ellen arched to the first touch of Kate's mouth on her breasts.

Ellen had become accustomed to making slow love with Stephanie, to eroticism sustained by periods of conversation, interruptions of mood. She was overwhelmed by the insistence of Kate's body and arms, the contrasting tenderness of Kate's hands so subtly caressing her breasts, her mouth that touched lightly in the hollow of her throat, her tongue sweetly stroking. Slowly, Kate's mouth moved down again, to her breasts. All thought vanished.

Kate turned over, to have Ellen on top of her, to clasp and caress the firm swelling of her hips. Ellen's thigh was between hers, and her own thighs closed convulsively; arousal had become an ache. With Anne, she would bring Anne's hand to her now, or turn over and press rhythmically until orgasm released her to continue making love ... Kate's hands slid down to curve around the thigh between hers. But Anne had never breathed like this, in such gasps.

Ellen lay on Kate's body breathing against her desire,

against the possessive hands undulating her hips. A thought passed through her, clear and desire-quenching: *I'm Anne.*

"Ellen."

Ellen looked at her.

"Ellen." Kate's eyes were closed. "Ellen..."

Ellen turned and pulled Kate on top of her, seeking the full substance of her.

Kate moved her body away. The soft cupping of her hand became her only connection to Ellen. She took her hand away only to know again the crisp softness warmly filling her palm; and yet a second time.

There was a sound—from Kate—as her fingertips touched, were enveloped in warm wetness. The fierce throbbing of her own flesh had eased; her mouth was dry with another want, single and specific.

"Ellen?"

Kate's eyes were burning, hypnotic. The moving, caressing fingertips created ever-widening erotic waves. Ellen answered helplessly, "Yes."

There was another sound—from Ellen—at the first touch of Kate's mouth.

In the ecstasy of tasting her, inhaling her, Kate knew a moment of fear that Ellen would not speak or somehow signal what she needed. Then she heard the sharp intakes of breath, felt the unmistakable stiffening of Ellen's body. Joyfully, slowly, Kate savored her, pressing the quivering thighs against her face.

She had not been with many women—and never with one who did not want her to readily come; repeatedly sensation intensified and then varied before Ellen realized that for now climax was secondary. She succumbed to sensation, became pure response. Tension became exquisitely unbearable. "Kate," she said in an agonized whisper. Then her body was gathered up into an intensity that ebbed only with the ebbing of orgasm.

She lay in Kate's arms, strength only slowly seeping back into her. Never had a woman's mouth so entirely possessed her.

Ellen's soft hands were warm pleasantness on her breasts,

but not arousal; feeling oddly satiated, Kate murmured, "I don't need... You were beautiful. I don't need anything else."

Remembering the wetness cool on her thigh as Kate had lifted her body from her, Ellen said simply, "I want to touch you."

Except for her hand which stroked in Ellen's hair, Kate received her caresses without moving. Ellen's fingers traced her breasts, Ellen's mouth took a nipple. Then, as if a veil had been suddenly stripped away, desire powerfully stirred. Kate pressed Ellen's mouth to her.

Ellen lightly stroked the smooth columns of thighs, gripping them again and again, pleasurably feeling their muscular strength. Questing fingers reached higher, explored hair finer than her own and thick—soft damp fur. Kate's legs jerked, and as Ellen's fingers caressed, her heels moved up and down the sheet, her legs opening with each rise and fall of her thighs. Ellen sat up, away from Kate's embrace, and bent to her.

She hung on a precipice of exquisite sensation, her hand clutching Ellen's hair. Tantalized beyond all endurance, she pulled Ellen's mouth away. "I can't," she gasped. "Not...like that."

"Then show me," Ellen said, coming to her, taking her in her arms. "Kate...want me..."

Again she felt Kate's wetness on her thigh, felt a tremor in Kate's body. She tightened her arms and strained up into her, as if to absorb her excitement.

Sensations dormant for long months had rekindled into brilliance. Ellen's arms fully embraced her, Ellen's body was satin under hers, Ellen's breath was hot against her throat. She felt soft lips press into her shoulder, the light imprint of teeth. Kate groaned from the satin friction, her body surging. Moments later she groaned again.

Her body arched into Kate's, Ellen felt the paroxysm, the sudden relaxation.

Soon afterward Kate managed to say, "You're wonderful."

"So are you." She loosened her grip, but held Kate closely during the long quiet moments that followed.

"Kleenex," Kate finally said. She added in a low mutter, "I've never been so wet."

Pleased, Ellen reached to the nightstand for the man-sized box of tissues.

Later Kate whispered, "Ellen?"

But Ellen, an arm across Kate, her head nestled into Kate's shoulder, was asleep. Anne had never liked sleeping close, even after lovemaking. Kate tightened her arm, drawing the warmth of Ellen even closer.

Kate was disturbed by the stirring of the warmth against her, then awakened by the chill of her body. In predawn light the digital clock read 5:22. Ellen had moved away but lay toward her on her side; in slumbering unawareness she shifted a breast from beneath her. Then she turned, her body curved away from Kate, arms outflung, hair in tangles, face buried in her pillow. The sweeping line of back was only partly exposed; other contours were suggested by the blanket. Irresistibly, hungrily, Kate ran a hand down the length of her. She stroked and kissed her back.

Ellen murmured part-pleasure, part-protest, but soon turned and gave Kate her arms. She received in return gentle caresses that warmed her and only gradually dissipated the somnolence of her body. Warmth became vague arousal, and memory returned of the pleasure she had known from Kate, body memory that rekindled desire.

Emboldened by her knowledge of Ellen, Kate took new and deeper pleasure in her, allowing herself to be led, rewarded by response even more quickly triggered. The tender prelude between them turned seamlessly into passion.

"Now," Ellen soon whispered, "now."

Kate gave all the pleasure she knew how to give, Ellen's gasps coming swiftly, her hips alternately rising then grinding into the bed.

Afterward in Kate's arms Ellen breathed "Kate... Kate," in thick-voiced exhaustion.

Profoundly content, Kate fell asleep.

Voices—the sound of the television—and the unaccustomed smell of coffee awakened Kate. Memory returned; and as she searched for something to cover herself, a feeling of bleakness enveloped her.

Ellen was in the living room curled up on the sofa in a blue robe, watching *Today*. Her glance swept the terry robe Kate wore; she raised her coffee cup in greeting. The gesture seemed ironic to Kate, and soberly, she nodded.

"Good morning." Ellen's voice was low and expressionless.

"Is it?"

Not very, Ellen thought. She said, "Coffee's ready."

Kate shook her head. "For once I wish I were in uniform. I can't go to work in the same clothes. Have to drive to Glendale."

"Glendale might as well be Bakersfield in rush hour traffic. Look." She ticked off on her fingers, "White blouse, gray slacks, green corduroy jacket. All you really need is another jacket. Borrow one of Stephanie's."

And why not, Ellen thought, glancing again at the familiar terry robe that covered a woman who was not Stephanie. She's already made use of everything else.

Kate plucked at the robe. "Even this is too snug."

"She's not that much smaller. She's got several jackets you could try. You'll get by."

She was pleased that Ellen did not consider Stephanie's superior slenderness of much consequence, and she knew she would not refuse if Stephanie's jackets fit her like a straight-jacket. "Why don't I cook breakfast? What do you like?"

Thinking churlishly that she could not stand cheeriness in the morning, Ellen held out her coffee cup. "Just coffee."

Kate took the cup and looked down at Ellen. "You know, I wasn't young when things changed in the sixties. All my upbringing, my influences, were from the fifties. I'm glad times have changed. There weren't many women in my life before Anne—none of them of any meaning. You're a different level of experience."

"That can be very dangerous to weak egos," Ellen said nastily, stung by Kate's words.

She had expected anything but this response. Not understanding how she had erred, Kate said in a hasty effort to atone, "But I admire you. I liked it...how you were... In every way. That's what I meant, all I meant. I thought you knew—could tell how much I liked it."

"At least you're honest." She muttered the words grudgingly, only partly mollified. She was angry that she seemed unable to prevent the opening of herself to this woman.

Kate exhaled, remembering her full schedule of activity for the day. "Time for me to be a cop again."

"I think I'll just go on being a loose-living sixties woman," Ellen said gratingly, anger rising again. "As well as your star witness."

Finally, she understood; and wondering how she could have been so stupid, Kate sat down beside her, careful not to touch her. "One time, Ellen, when I was off duty, I found a woman lying on the ground with a crowd of people standing around just staring at her. She'd been hit by a girder from a highrise, both arms smashed, internal injuries, bleeding—she couldn't be touched or moved. It was raining hard, the rain just pouring down on her. She was unconscious, but I spread my raincoat over her, I didn't care about her blood on it or anything else except she was helpless... Then somebody else thought to hold an umbrella over her till an ambulance—"

"Am I the raincoat?" Ellen interrupted, smiling. "Or the umbrella?"

Kate said, "This morning when I woke up, the first thing I felt was lousy. What happened between us was because you'd felt sorry for me—"

"That's not true," Ellen interrupted vehemently. "That's the *last* reason—"

"Then the next thing I thought," Kate continued, "was that I'd done something to betray Anne."

"I felt like shit this morning," Ellen said quietly, her voice low and tense. "But you had no reason to feel bad, Kate—not for a second."

"Neither of us did, that's the point. But it was my first

instinct, too. Last night was unconnected to anything else in our lives, Ellen. It was—"

Ellen reached to Kate, touched her cheek. "At least I have good taste in the people I find out in the rain."

Kate smiled at Ellen. "You know, I can't imagine why I ever thought you were anything like Anne. You're not—at all."

"Yesterday was a bad emotional time for you. Anybody who resembled Anne might've triggered... what I did."

"But that's what I mean. You really *don't* look like her. Not at all."

Immensely pleased, Ellen touched Kate's cheek again.

Chapter 13

Taylor said, "Know how you can tell it's Sunday?"

Kate sighed and did not answer. She sat at her desk sorting through a day's accumulation of paper, and reading crime scene reports and interviews with Modern Office employees.

"The niggers are in church, the Jews are in Palm Springs, the beaners are fixing their cars, and the Polacks think it's Tuesday."

Kate sighed again. "The autopsy report. Give."

"Hey, I'm part Polack," Taylor protested, "I gotta right." He looked injured. "You ever gonna laugh at one of my jokes?"

"Never. Why do you keep trying?"

"One of these days I'm gonna make you laugh." Taylor dropped the report on Kate's desk and trudged back to his own paper-strewn desk to pick up a ringing phone.

Taylor had attended the autopsy of Fergus Parker; Kate scanned the preliminary report, picked out its conclusion: death by cardiac puncturation. Entrance wound in the left ventricle, flooding of the pericardial cavity exacerbated by the victim's movements.

She skimmed Fergus Parker's vital statistics, noting only that he was five feet nine inches and weighed two hundred and thirty-two pounds. Aortic arteriosclerosis present. Distended urinary bladder. External hemorrhoids. Obesity. Semen level normal. Fingernail scrapings negative. Blood and all blood samples O Positive, all preliminary tests normal.

But there was one new element, and Kate recorded it in her notebook: among undigested food in Fergus Parker's stomach was several ounces of red wine. She sat tapping her pen against her chin, thinking of Helen Parker's remark that Fergus Parker would drink a little red wine if he were celebrating something ...

She read over other test reports. A partial palm print had been lifted from the glass coffee pot, value pending. Cigarette ash was found along with cigar ash in Fergus Parker's ashtray. Of the employees past and present, only ex-employee James W. Scott had a prior, 1978. ADW, the assault on his wife, the deadly weapon a poker, charges dropped. Probability zero there, she decided, tugging her cuffs down below the sleeves of her too-tight jacket.

How could anyone leave Ellen O'Neil under these circumstances, she thought as she organized the reports. No matter how important that seminar was, Stephanie should have known to stay with her. Or she should have taken Ellen with her.

She picked up the photographs. After several minutes of scrutiny she spread the closeups of the corpse over her desk and looked carefully at the wound, at the curved and faceted handle of the protruding knife. The autopsy report had listed measurements of the wound, its size slightly larger than the blade—normal for a double-edged weapon. The wound was clean, no tear. The slight curve of the handle was up and down, not sideways, the heavy handle almost perfectly squared with the body.

She stood and pushed her chair back, and using a pocket

knife she kept in her desk, feinted in the air with both right and left-handed thrusts, trying to duplicate the entry of the knife into Fergus Parker. Standing at varied distances from an imaginary victim, she could only make the knife go in at a downward angle. And it seemed that plunging the knife with an upward thrust would create a slashing, jagged entry—when the actual wound was a clean puncture. She stood beside the chair and plunged her knife into her imaginary victim from the side. That worked—if she cocked her wrist at an awkward angle and held the handle sideways to duplicate the position of the curved handle.

Taylor got up from his desk and strolled over. "Kate, maybe I can help you stab whoever you got sitting in your chair."

Kate chuckled. "Fergus Parker."

"I figured."

Kate showed him the photographs and demonstrated the problem again. Taylor tried a few experimental thrusts of his own.

"Kate, what about this?" He stood behind the desk chair and plunged the knife downward.

"Good idea, Ed. It would explain why he didn't struggle. Sit down and let me try. You're more Fergus Parker's size."

"Thanks a lot, partner." Taylor sat. "And be careful with that blade, will you?"

Kate dangled the pocket knife playfully. "This? Don't worry, it doesn't slice baloney."

She took her place behind Taylor, held the blade over his head, plunged it in an arc that ended at Taylor's blue plaid lapel. "Closest yet, Ed. But look at the angle." She held the blade poised against Taylor. "Still upward. And I think it would tear the body. And splatter blood all over the killer's arms."

"Maybe. What about the victim standing? Fell back into the chair?"

"That was Everson's theory, remember? Let's try."

A few minutes later Taylor said, "It's possible. If he stood there leaning back with his chest puffed out and said here, stab me."

"There's still suicide."

"You don't believe that any more than me. Doesn't figure, the coroner doesn't think so, either."

"Right, it's not likely. Unless we discover something totally off the wall." Kate stacked the photographs. "I'm waiting for a phone call from Philadelphia, Gail Freeman's checking out a call Fergus Parker received from there yesterday morning. I'll meet you at Modern Office. We get anything on the cigarette butt yet?"

"Nope. Nice jacket."

Kate tugged again at her cuffs. "You really like it?"

"Fits nice. Like a glove."

Kate grinned. "Too much like one. Think I'll take it back."

"Kidding, aren't you? You're in a hell of a good mood this morning, Kate. Bet you got laid last night."

"Nope," Kate said cheerfully. Last night had been many things—but she would never term it that.

Her phone rang. "Detective Delafield? This is Wesley Miller in Philadelphia."

"Yes sir. Are you the individual who talked to Fergus Parker yesterday morning?"

"Yes I did, called Fergus at seven sharp. Just like I told him I would. I understand from Gail you're actually heading up the investigation. Quite a responsibility. Very progressive city you have there."

The effervescence of Kate's mood vanished. "Lieutenant David Bell is available to give you my qualifications, Mr. Miller, if that's a concern to you." She concentrated on the pleasantness of her tone. "None of us at LAPD like to work with unqualified people, whoever they may be."

"Yes indeed, and I do admire that. I do admire your attitude about that. Wish more people in power thought that way. Gail speaks very highly of you. Now, how can I help you?" Wesley Miller spoke easily, his tone bland.

"Your conversation with Fergus Parker, what was the substance of it?"

"Miss, uh, Detective Delafield, can I have your assurance it'll be kept confidential?"

She made no attempt to soften the hard edges of her tone.

"No. Not if it's relevant to the solution and eventual resolution of this case."

"Oh, I agree with that. I just don't think it will be. I don't see how it could be. Let me explain. I called Fergus to offer him a new position. He was to head up all the company operations west of the Mississippi. But you see, now that he's, ah, not on board, we've had to, ah, reshuffle our plans. And it wouldn't do for, ah, certain people in the organization to know what we had in mind, they wouldn't understand why they weren't chosen in the first place, won't be chosen now."

"I see. Whose decision was it to offer this position?"

"It was my recommendation. But in business this kind of decision is never made autonomously." Wesley Miller's tone was condescending. "I had enthusiastic approvals from the entire executive board including Jonathon. Jonathon Wagner, our president."

"Enthusiastic approvals on what basis?"

"The firmest basis." Wesley Miller's voice strengthened. "The profit of western operations rose fourteen percent the past two years. The numbers from our other regional centers showed a decline."

Numbers, Kate thought. Always numbers. "Did you speak with anyone out here about this promotion? Ask their opinion of Fergus Parker?"

"Certainly not, Detective Delafield. The business world is not a democracy. Our country's democracy is not a democracy."

"Thank you Mr. Miller, but at least one of your employees found a way to vote. Did Fergus Parker accept the job?"

"Yes, yes he did. With a few provisos."

"Which were?"

"Oh, that he'd have some autonomy in certain areas of hiring and firing, that he'd still be based in L.A."

"And did you agree to his conditions?"

"Substantially. With a quibble here and there."

"Exactly what were his conditions and what were your quibbles?"

"Detective, I can't see how this is relevant to anything, the information is confidential—"

"Mr. Miller." Kate stared unseeingly at the drab clutter of the detectives' room, concentrating on reading the cadences and tones of Wesley Miller's voice. "Mr. Miller, let me put it to you this way. I'm conducting a murder investigation out here, and a good part of that inquiry involves the motive for killing Fergus Parker. An employee who learned he would be dismissed from the company—"

"Even so—"

"Let me put it this way, Mr. Miller." Men in power, she thought in disgust. "We have a fine working arrangement with the Philadelphia police. You can cooperate and answer my questions fully, or I can arrange to have my counterparts there—"

"Madam, it was never my intention to interfere with your investigation. We're absolutely appalled back here by this incredible event, the loss of so valuable a man. I'm sure you can understand that I have to consider the best interests of the company ... The first thing Fergus wanted was final say on manpower levels and all job assignments in Los Angeles." Wesley Miller's voice had changed from sharpness to caution.

"Isn't that partly Gail Freeman's territory?"

"I see you've informed yourself about the office there. It's primarily Gail's territory, but it wasn't really a problem. In areas of disagreement we'd have simply arbitrated the matter here without either man knowing. We do that more often than subordinates realize. But Fergus also demanded that Freeman be fired. Of course I couldn't agree to that, I explained how extremely careful we have to be with black terminations. Even with the Reagan presidency. Particularly when a man's record has been as exemplary as Freeman's. We still need to act with caution in the area of equal—"

"What commitment did you make about Mr. Freeman?"

Wesley Miller cleared his throat with a protracted har-rumph. "I agreed we'd try to work out an, ah, attractive transfer opportunity."

Simply move a cog to another part of the machine, she thought, recording the answer in her notes. "What else, Mr. Miller?"

"I presume you've met Guy Adams, nephew of our founder. Done an outstanding job wherever we've sent him, but apparently there'd been some conflict with Fergus. I told Fergus, and I was very adamant about this, even though old Guy Adams passed on some months back there's no way we can simply kick his nephew out the door, I mean, how would it look?"

"What commitment did you make about Mr. Adams?"

Wesley Miller harrumphed again. "Fergus finally backed off some and said he wanted him at least out of his territory, maybe we could bury him some place like the Savannah office. I agreed to discuss it with Jonathon and see what we could work out."

"Do you feel Fergus Parker was justified in either of those demands?"

"Justified?" Wesley Miller was indignant. "Justice doesn't apply here, madam. It's a maxim of management that a man has to have loyalty and support from the men around him. By the same token, it's a definite reflection on the two men who didn't have the good judgment to work out a satisfactory relationship with a man in the position of Fergus Parker."

"Anything else you discussed?"

"He wanted some say in naming his successor. And said he'd be making some key changes in his own sales managers in the coming months."

"Did he say what those changes would be?"

"Not specifically. He mentioned Fred Grayson and Harley Burton as the ones he had in mind. We always discussed his decisions about his people, of course, but it was pretty much his prerogative to operate as he wished in his own area, so long as he kept turning in good profit numbers."

"Anything else?" She began a fresh page of notes.

"Not really. We discussed remuneration, but I don't think—" Wesley Miller hurriedly amended, "Do you need to know about that?"

"Not at the moment."

"And the effective date of his promotion. We agreed on March thirty-first. And that he should travel around his new territory immediately after—"

"Thank you, Mr. Miller. One more question. Will you be taking any action now about Mr. Freeman or Mr. Adams?"

"Well, possibly Guy. Now that his uncle—now that we're under no obligation to—well, public relations is an expensive proposition even in the best economic times. But Gail—well, if we have to have a black manager, L.A.'s a good city, very liberal and all, more accepting—well, you know. And continuity's very important till we adjust to this very tragic—I think you can see now why I was concerned about confidentiality."

"You have my word on that if your information proves irrelevant. Mr. Miller, I may call you again with further questions?"

"Ah, one thing. We're discussing a replacement for Fergus, we're all wondering back here who you might've eliminated as suspects so that—"

"I can't discuss the investigation," Kate said curtly. "I'm sure you understand."

"Oh certainly," Wesley Miller said resignedly. "I hope you'll soon—"

"I'm sure we will. Good day, sir."

Chapter 14

Kate reviewed her caseload, thoughts of Ellen O'Neil frequently intruding on her concentration. As she drove to Modern Office, she pondered the few personal facts she had learned about Ellen that morning. Six years with an alcoholic lover. Within a month of that breakup, the death of her father. Stephanie Hale had come on the scene soon afterward; six months later Ellen had quit a responsible job and spent the next year and a half helping Stephanie Hale write an economics text, acting as her research assistant.

Kate had asked, "Aren't books on economic theory soon obsolete?"

"Yes, usually. But this one's a study of information used to develop and formulate theory."

That would put an owl to sleep, Kate had thought. "Well, I

hope she dedicated it to you."

"Oh no, she couldn't do that... that would be—It's not the kind of book you dedicate, anyway. But I'll get a nice note on the acknowledgement page."

Kate turned onto Merlin Street, parked, and looked with pleasure at the oak trees. She got out and locked the Plymouth. *A year and a half of her life. For a nice note on the acknowledgement page.*

"Hi, Cagney! Where ya been?"

"Good morning, Miss Markham." Kate waved at Judy Markham, who flung back her blonde hair, breasts bouncing, and buzzed her through the lobby doors.

She stopped at the crime scene. The stench of alcohol had heightened several fold over the past hours. Breathing with difficulty, she examined Fergus Parker's desk and chair and credenza. The red wine listed on the autopsy report meant that somewhere amid the smashed glass of Fergus Parker's bar were pieces of a wine bottle. Also a cork, if the bottle had been opened yesterday morning. And the wrapping from around the cork. And wine glasses. Possibly that was why the killer, a coffee drinker, had not brought coffee into Fergus Parker's office—he and his victim were drinking wine. As the host, Fergus Parker would probably have opened the bottle—but if he had not ... There should be fingerprints, regardless; either Fergus Parker's or someone else's. The bottle and glasses could be reconstructed. Baker was the best fingerprint technician in the division. If there were prints of value in all that glass, Baker would find them.

She closed the door quietly after her and glanced down the hall. Guy Adams' office door was open. Guy Adams, who was infatuated with Ellen, she remembered. She turned and walked the other way, past the conference room, glancing into offices as she walked. Gretchen Phillips, chin held pensively in a hand tipped with coral fingernails, stared into space, smoke curling up from an ashtray hidden by mounds of paper. Duane

Fletcher, gesticulating with a cigarette, talked on the phone in high-pitched enthusiasm. Harley Burton's office was empty; he was next door arguing with a stony-faced Fred Grayson.

She paused. Both men looked up with irritated expressions. Reaching toward an ashtray, Fred Grayson growled, "You arrest anybody yet?"

She shook her head and walked on. Grayson, she noted, had abandoned Tiparillos.

Kate slowed, hands in her jacket pockets, to peer into Ellen O'Neil's office. She was on the phone, and waggled three fingers at Kate, then used them to cover the receiver. "Nice jacket," she whispered, and grinned.

"A friend gave me the use of it," she said solemnly, and winked, and strolled into Gail Freeman's office.

"Good morning." Gail Freeman rose to shake hands. "Did Wesley Miller call?"

"Yes, and thank you for your good work."

"Thank Ellen. She got on the problem like a bulldog." Kate said, smiling, "Miss O'Neil seems very capable for a new person."

"Terrific. Sharp and quick."

"Yes." She added in an objective tone, "A very attractive person."

To her surprise, Freeman shrugged. "Guess I'm old-fashioned. I like to work with women like her, but that's all. I admire women like you, like her. Women who can fix their own cars, that sort of thing. Forgive me, but I wouldn't marry you."

Kate chuckled. "That's all right. But I think Ellen—" She caught herself. "Ellen O'Neil doesn't look like the mechanic type to me."

"Not literally. I just meant she's very much her own person."

"Do you think so? I've found people can be in control only of certain facets of their lives."

"I suppose you're right." Gail Freeman grinned. "I'll confess I'm not only a chauvinist, but a racist. I adore dark-skinned women." He turned, took the picture of his family from the credenza and displayed it for Kate. "My wife, see how beautiful she is? I think God made her the loveliest of any human creature."

"Beautiful indeed, Mr. Freeman," Kate said truthfully, gazing at the chocolate-skinned woman in the photo. "Your daughters are also very pretty."

"Thank you. My family is the world—" He broke off. "How's the case coming? Any suspects yet? Other than me?"

"Sure," Kate said, smiling.

"Seriously, is there anything I can tell the employees? You can imagine how they feel, all the rumors flying around. The idea of a killer in our office—"

"Yes, I can well imagine. There aren't any definite views of what constitutes a killer's mentality, but based on my experience—this is by no means an official position of any kind—this appears to be an impulse crime, we aren't dealing with a homicidal maniac likely to commit multiple crimes. All I can give you to tell your people is that we're working on every possible lead, we welcome any information anyone might have. And we hope to make an arrest soon."

"Sounds impressive," Freeman said lightly.

Kate smiled. "Best I can do." She glanced at her watch. "I see it's almost lunch time here. I'll finish looking over the files in the conference room. Then interview Billie Sullivan."

"Does that mean I can fire her afterward?"

"You seem very anxious."

"I don't trust her. I want her out of here. I think she's got something up her sleeve."

Taylor was pacing the conference room with buoyant steps. "All kinds of news, Kate. We broke the MacKenzie case. Picked up two Latinos doing their act in Ohrbach's parking lot. One of 'em was rearranging the victim's skull when Forster and Deems rolled up. One's already blaming the other for MacKenzie. The Lieutenant's hopping and skipping with joy. Been a year since he got his mug on TV. Maybe he'll get off our backs for a while, all the followup paper—"

"Don't hold your breath. He's moving to Foothill in June, remember? He'll keep his nose squeaky clean till then." She was leafing through the personnel file on Billie Sullivan, imagining Lieutenant David Bell's tenor voice lowered to factual grimness for the benefit of radio station reporters' tape recorders, the boyish features drawn into solemnity for the television cameras from all seven local stations. Not for her; never would she be interested in the PR of police work. She said to Taylor, "What else've you got?"

"ID on the cigarette butt. Carlton."

"Terrific," she said ironically. "That narrows it down only to Guy Adams, Gretchen Phillips, Fred Grayson and Harley Burton." But Taylor was still grinning. "We luck out?"

"Yep. Good ABO reading. Blood type B."

Kate smiled and nodded, pleased at the unusual blood type lifted from the saliva on the cigarette butt. "This one may be solved by the lab, the way it looks right now."

"Circumstantial? Shit. Ohrbach's this morning, that's my idea of a good case."

Kate said absently, flipping through her notebook for a note she had made yesterday, "They convict more and more on circumstantial, Ed."

"Yeah, and the appeals take into the next century."

She had found her note, and was uninterested in pursuing this tired subject. "You mentioned a coffee mug you saw in the kitchen yesterday, English hunting scene on it. Empty, you said. What did you mean by empty?"

There was a pause. "An absence of liquid, Kate."

Obligingly, she chuckled. "Was it bone dry? As in washed and dried? Or with dregs in it that sat all night and dried out?"

Taylor ran his hands through his thin blond hair. "Shit I see what you mean. No, it wasn't bone dry, I don't remember if the liquid was fresh or not quite dried out from the day before."

"Filmed over? Any residue on the bottom of the mug?"

"God damn it, I can't remember. Shit." His voice was heavy with self-reproach. "Whose mug?"

"Harley Burton. Saw it in his office yesterday."

"Shit. That was the other piece of news, Kate. The partial on the coffee pot—his. God damn it."

"Relax, Ed. We're not mind readers."

"Second thing I've blown. Yesterday the crime scene—"

"Forget it. All of us do it, it's tough to guess what's significant in a case like this one. Even the print—could be days old. We have to establish who washes the coffee pot and when they do it."

"Let me handle that, check it out."

Kate knew that yesterday she would have pilloried Taylor for carelessness; in recent months she had been a driven perfectionist, a misery to work with. Taylor would never know how much he owed to Ellen O'Neil for this newly rational perspective.

"Harley Burton is a possible," she said. "The one who seems most doubtful is Guy Adams. Unless Fergus Parker filled him in on a scheme he had to ship him off to the boondocks. And I don't see what difference that would make to Adams—he's worked all over the country. He's got the weakest motive of anybody so far. Friction, yes. But Fergus Parker didn't do the things to Adams he did to people who worked directly for him. I know he referred to Adams as a fag, but I can't see that being enough to kill anybody."

"It would be for me," Taylor growled. "I got nothing against it," he said with a quick glance at Kate, "to each his own. But anybody ever suggested I had a limp wrist, I'd paint cement red with the bastard's face."

Kate thought of Gretchen Phillips, her struggle for her success. How can women ever be equal, she thought, when the accusation of femininity is always the ultimate insult to men?

Taylor said, "Funny, I thought we'd make a quick collar here and never put the MacKenzie case to bed. Besides Harley Burton, we got any other good possibles?"

Kate's sigh was partly a groan. "With the exception of Ellen O'Neil and Helen Parker, everybody I've talked to so far."

"Take 'em all in for heavy duty interrogation?"

"Not yet. I want to hear what Billie Sullivan has to say. Right now from a physical standpoint—if we go by the time element we worked out yesterday—Duane Fletcher isn't likely. He's more your typical out-of-shape, middle-age spread executive type. And Gretchen Phillips doesn't look likely. But Fred Grayson and Harley Burton and Guy Adams and Gail Freeman—all good physical specimens. Especially Freeman—small, wiry, athletic. Except for Adams, all with very strong motives."

"This case reminds me of that movie, all those people on a train, all suspects. Turns out all of 'em did it."

"*Murder on the Orient Express.* Agatha Christie." Kate was smiling; Anne had loved the movie.

"Maybe all of 'em did do it, Kate." Taylor was serious; his voice had risen in eagerness. "Or at least a couple. They all have a motive?"

"Motive, malice, intent. All of them from similar backgrounds, too—education, intelligence, moral values—except maybe Fred Grayson. Grayson has to take off his Ku Klux Klan hood to come to work."

"I don't mind a little prejudice," Taylor said.

"I wish I'd known about him before, you could've interviewed him instead of me. Enough to gag a maggot."

Taylor accepted the insult with a good-natured shrug. "My theory, Kate—what do you really think? Somebody held Fergus Parker's arms, somebody else plowed him. Wouldn't that explain the stab wound? And no struggle?"

"It's possible, Ed. But then we have all kinds of problems with Ellen O'Neil's story. And the psychology's all wrong. These people aren't roving thugs like the two we got this morning."

"Amateur City." Taylor exhaled noisily. "I'm leaving, gotta put the MacKenzie case to bed. I'll be glad to get outta here permanently, back on the street. My calm dignity act is a fat bore. These white-collar business types are one big yawn."

"It doesn't seem very likely these white-collar types would get together and commit premeditated murder."

"Kate, we've seen some pretty strange—"

"I know, Ed. I'm not dismissing any possibilities. See you later."

Chapter 15

Painted British flags festooned *The White Cliffs of Dover*, a blue and white A-frame with a bright red door. The bar and tables and chairs were of coarse-grained wood; the lighting was subdued. The place was crowded but quiet, filled with murmuring conversations.

"Ellen, this isn't where I'd have taken you," Guy said apologetically. "It's pretty masculine here, sort of male-clubby."

"I like it," Ellen declared, thinking that Stephanie would judge it low class, would sneer at the homely interior, the roughly dressed customers.

Stephanie had called the office that morning; they had spoken briefly, Ellen pleading the press of work (which was true) and a deadline on a report (which was not true). Conscience-stricken at her betrayal of fidelity to Stephanie, she was certain that she would give herself away, certain that Stephanie would somehow hear the guilt in her voice and know that she had spent the night giving comfort and intimacy to another woman.

"It's a regular British pub," Guy said. "Most of the patrons have their own mugs, see?" Above the bar, on a long double rack, hung dozens of beer mugs, all sizes and styles, some plain, some pewter, some glistening painted porcelain. "Nice custom, isn't it? We'd never take our customers here, but everybody in the office loves the place. And they've sort of adopted us. This table's always reserved at lunch. And one of the dart boards."

Guy was on one side of her, Gail on the other. The round table, large enough for eight, was close to the bar and next to the game area. Behind them the billiard table was deserted. To taunts from the bartender, a paunchy man in khaki pants and a pea jacket intermittently hurled bullet-like darts at one of two black and white sectioned dart boards.

"It was nice of you to ask me here." Ellen had raised her voice to include everyone at the table. She suspected this invitation had been a ploy of Guy's—she could hardly refuse an offer to join all the managers for lunch. "You've been very kind to me," she said. "Very good about … everything."

"We try harder," Duane Fletcher said. "The quality goes in before the name goes on."

Forewarned about Duane Fletcher, Ellen chuckled.

"You may not believe this," Gretchen Phillips said, smiling affectionately at Duane Fletcher, "but Duane's name is actually Granny Goose."

"No, he's the Aqua Velva man," Harley Burton said heartily. "There's something about an Aqua Velva man."

"A little dab'll do ya." Gail Freeman directed a playful punch at Duane Fletcher.

"Please don't squeeze the Charmin," Duane Fletcher squealed amid the laughter, avoiding Gail Freeman's feint.

A leather-aproned waiter brought a tray of heavy glass beer mugs foamed well above the rim. "It's Miller time," Fred Grayson said, to more laughter.

Guy Adams raised his mug and said with exaggerated irony, "To a better Modern Office."

"To the late unlamented," Gail Freeman offered.

"Everything you never wanted in a boss, and less." Duane Fletcher clinked mugs with Gail.

Harley Burton said cheerfully, "Bet he's already general manager of hell."

"All that lard should burn forever," Gretchen Phillips said.

Laughing helplessly, Ellen took refuge in her beer mug, the smell pleasantly acrid, the coolness wet and sharp.

"Another toast," Gail Freeman said. "To whoever did it."

Movement at the table stopped. Ellen realized numbly that she could be sitting with a murderer. The person who had been in the office with her yesterday, who had plunged a blade into Fergus Parker's heart. She looked from Guy Adams to Gretchen Phillips to Fred Grayson, to Harley Burton, to Duane Fletcher, watching their stares freeze on Gail Freeman. His gaze traversed his companions coolly, and he continued in a soft voice, "I hope the cops give up soon and get back to more urgent concerns, like giving tickets."

Duane Fletcher said, "I'm Chiquita Banana and I'm here to say that bananas have to ripen in a certain way."

Ellen burst into laughter. Accompanying loud laughter from around the table broke the tension.

"Guy sweetie?" Gretchen Phillips' smile was coaxing. "Why don't you give me one of Harley's cigarettes? Preferably without a lecture. Then let's win more of his money."

"Not today." Harley Burton's tone was abrupt. "Don't much feel like playing today."

"Nor me," Guy Adams said, his face sobering.

"Terrific," Gretchen Phillips said imperturbably. "Best time to take you both on."

"You don't need any advantage," Harley Burton growled.

"Guy sweetie? A cigarette please?"

"Sure, Gretchen." Guy extracted a cigarette from his inside blazer pocket, lit it, and with a charming smile tucked it between Gretchen Phillips' lips. She patted his cheek. Ellen watched them with pleasure, admiring their grace and beauty.

Gail got up and went over to the bar to pick up the darts. Fred Grayson said to Ellen, "We put up a dollar a game. Total points takes the money."

Ellen watched Gail draw each dart back behind his ear, launch it in a swift graceful arc. Harley Burton was next, hurling his in a single powerful motion, rattling the dart board against the wall. Coming back to the table, he tossed a dollar down with a snort of disgust.

"Try accuracy instead of velocity," Fred Grayson taunted.

"It's both," Harley Burton grunted. He said to Ellen, "Played baseball in college, hell of a fastball. Only pitch I had, could fire that damn ball through a needle in those days."

"I believe you," Ellen murmured, gazing at his bulging arms and chest.

Their food arrived, shaved roast beef on two halves of a thick sourdough roll. Guy spread his sandwich with horseradish so pungent the odor made Ellen's eyes water. Gail cut his sandwich into eighths, then bit fastidiously into one of his mini-snacks. Ellen ate her sandwich with enjoyment, listening to shop talk, some of it already familiar terminology.

"Tell me," she asked, her eyes fixed on the center of the table, her question directed to no one in particular, "the people in Philadelphia—doesn't it matter to them what goes on out here? What kind of man Fergus Parker was?"

"The eastern people," Harley Burton answered, "they come out once, twice a year for a few days. We send 'em back wined, dined, entertained."

"And unenlightened," Gretchen Phillips added, taking a bite from her sandwich.

Fred Grayson had scowled at the candor of his fellow managers. But he said, "Numbers. All they ever want is the numbers. How we did against Apex. What our market share is, how we plan to improve it."

Guy Adams' face was somber. "All the direction and energy went out of the company when my uncle died. All the moral force. Bookkeepers, accountants." His voice was bitter. "A caretaker management for a once great company. A company that's become a still-life."

Fred Grayson got up. Before each toss of a dart he swung his arm back and forth in a vigorous pendulum, then sighted along it as if over the sights of a rifle. Each dart traveled in a

swift straight trajectory, crowding around the bullseye area.
"Not bad, Fred." Gretchen Phillips retrieved the darts and
walked quickly to the line. She released her darts quickly, in
an economy of motion, each soft toss winging straight into the
bullseye.

"Tough," muttered Harley Burton. "Women's equality is
one thing. Damn superiority's something else."

Guy asked Ellen, "Would you like to try?"

"I'll leave it to you athletes," Ellen said, smiling at Gretchen
Phillips.

"Me too." Duane Fletcher drained his beer mug. "Let it be
Lowenbrau for Duane. Good to the last drop. The champagne
of bottled beers. Put a little weekend in your—"

"Stuff it, Duane," Fred Grayson said through a bite of his
sandwich.

Guy took his place behind the line. In a blur of movement
Ellen did not completely follow, a dart flew straight and true and
thudded just inside the bullseye. Gretchen Phillips applauded.
Ellen watched him, her eyes following the seam of shirt that
outlined his shoulders; the planes of his back down to his hips;
his long legs. He was extraordinarily attractive, for a man.

Guy finished his darts, the others thrown not nearly so
accurately as the first, and tossed his dollar down onto the table.
With a grin and a wink at Ellen, Gretchen Phillips picked up all
the money. Gail pulled the darts out of the board for another
game. They continued to play as they finished lunch, Gail barely
outpointing Gretchen Phillips in the next contest.

"Sorry boys," Gretchen Phillips said, "I have to get back.
Got to call East before they all leave."

Scraping his chair back to get up, Gail said, "Back to the
not-so-tender mercies of Detective Delafield."

Ellen started guiltily; she had been remembering Kate
Delafield, her thoughts intimate and lingering. She said, half-
humorously, "She's very good at her job."

Six pairs of eyes looked at her. Disconcerted, she leaned
over and picked up her purse.

Chapter 16

Billie Sullivan called from the storage closet in her office, "Gimme two more seconds."

Kate caught glimpses of stringy red hair and a pink man-tailored blouse, its tail hanging out over a green skirt so wrinkled the pattern was indiscernible. Sitting down in the single chair in front of Billie Sullivan's desk, she watched, fascinated, as from the closet into a huge cardboard box were flung nylon stockings, tennis shoes, a sweater, two candles, four cans of Budweiser, a pillow, a clock radio, a set of wind chimes, and a sack of pistachio nuts.

Billie Sullivan emerged from the closet smacking her hands together in satisfaction, and moved to her desk in liquid loping strides. She folded herself into her chair. "So grill me, lady copper."

She was the thinnest woman Kate had ever seen, the bones of the arms she propped on the desk protruding whitely through the skin. She looked at Kate with raised reddish eyebrows, neither green eye precisely focused. Kate asked, "How come you're packing?"

"I figure that dink manager's gonna toss my ass any second."

"Why would he want to do that?" Kate's voice was expressionless.

"I do even less around here than Fred Grayson. The world champion brown-noser and dumb shit."

A woman with nothing whatever to lose, Kate saw. "Hasn't he been sales manager here a number of years?" She stuffed her hands into the pockets of her undersize jacket and arranged herself comfortably in the chair. For now she would take no notes.

"So what if he has? He's an asshole. And *dumb?* I bet his wife has to write directions on her body."

Kate hastily removed a hand from a pocket to rub it across her grin. "Miss Sullivan—"

"I won't talk to anyone that calls me that." Her tone was adamant. "I'm Billie."

"Billie," she conceded. "Who would want to kill your boss?"

She gritted her teeth against the screeching laugh. "You want I should list them in order?"

"It would be helpful," Kate said drily.

Several of the fingernails Billie Sullivan tapped on the desk were broken, the sharp edges unfiled. "Hard to say," she said finally. "Harley Burton's number one easy if he knew how much shit the boss actually did him. But I'd have to say ... Well, the boss all but pulled out his cock and pissed all over Gail Freeman."

Billie Sullivan picked up a desk dictionary and hurled it into the cardboard box. Kate waited.

"The boss did everything we could think of. Believe me, together we could be pretty cute. Only a matter of time before we figured a way to airmail his ass."

"Why do *you* dislike Mr. Freeman?"

"Not because he's colored, if that's your drift," she said

immediately. "The boss and dumbshit Grayson, they hate blacks—but I don't. Colored, female—I figure that's a trade-off." She gyrated on her chair, pulling bony fingers through her hair. "Gail Freeman bullshits everybody that works for him. Claims we all do something *valuable*, for chrissakes." Her tone was withering. "A boss gave me that snowjob just *once*. Before I found out what a stinking cesspool business really is. Men," she sneered, "it's their fucking world, all their fun and games. Men have it *all* and they aren't about to give it up, I don't care what kind of stupid movements come along to try and stop them. All the bastards ever want to do is kill each other and fuck every woman they see."

Kate cleared her throat and said mildly, "Don't you think Mr. Freeman is at least sincere?"

"Sincere? *Sincere?*" Her out-of-focus eyes glared at Kate. "What does *sincere* have to do with anything? Lady copper, you wear a gun?"

Warily, Kate nodded. "Regulations."

"I wish to Christ I could. Wear it right out on my hip like a cowboy. Right where everybody can see it. Eat or get eaten, that's all there is, nothing more. Five minutes after you're dead nobody knows your name."

Cynical as any cop, Kate thought, watching her.

"Gail Freeman took away the boss's fun, lots of his games. Made the boss have to *think*. Every change he made, the boss had to call in brown-noser Grayson and learn all about it so nobody could get a leg up on him. He *hated* Gail Freeman."

"Sounds like your boss had more motive to murder Gail Freeman than the other way around," Kate commented as she took out her notebook and consulted her brief profile of Billie Sullivan. "Billie, you've worked here three years, two months. Two years longer than any other job. Why did you get along so well with Fergus Parker?"

"Tell you a story. Few months back, Pete Webber wised up and quit. Gave the boss a gift, a shovel with a red ribbon on it. Said the boss should dig up his own mother and screw her too, she was the only person he hadn't done it to, what difference did it make she was dead?"

156 Katherine V. Forrest

"You're making that up," Kate said.

Screeching with laughter, Billie Sullivan shook a cigarette from a pack of Benson & Hedges. "Yeah, but it's a neat story, right? I knew exactly what I had to deal with in the boss. Other bosses I had, they were assholes too but they'd do nice things once in a while, help somebody, give money to charity, that kind of shit. Not the boss." She exhaled smoke in a thin jet, placed a blade sharp elbow on the desk, and cupped her chin. "I could depend on the boss to be a total stinko."

Kate smiled. "It's nice to have consistency in this world. Who's number two on your list?"

"The brown-noser," she said promptly. "You know where you stand with him, too. Absolutely nowhere. If he was going down for the last time, had to decide between a rope and life preserver, he'd drown."

Kate smiled again. "How could a successful manager like Fred Grayson be indecisive?"

"Easy. Real easy." Billie Sullivan flicked ash in the direction of a battered metal ashtray. "He didn't used to be indecisive. The boss and me, we punched him into the perfect company man. Anybody can do it—even to you, lady copper. You make a decision and your boss stands up in front of other people and says you're wrong and stupid besides."

Kate said evenly, "That would happen exactly once."

Billie Sullivan surveyed her with a glance. "Yeah, maybe not you. Maybe not some other people. But the brown-noser caved right in. A man's got to stand up at least once and put his balls on the table, right? That asshole never had the guts to stand up *once*." Her voice was vibrant with contempt. "In return for giving up his balls and licking the boss's ass, the boss kept him around and made all his decisions for him."

"You seem to have a special distaste for Mr. Grayson."

"Wouldn't you? How can anybody give his balls away? God damn it, if I was a man I'd run this fucking world."

Indeed you might, Kate thought. "Why would Fred Grayson want to kill the man who was taking care of him?"

"Oh come on." Billie Sullivan bared her teeth in a humorless grin. "You're a woman. Don't shit me. Don't let on you don't understand all about getting fucked and being taken care of. How it feels, what you think about it."

Kate cleared her throat. "Who's next?"

"Gretchen, I suppose. Only because she didn't know how well off she was."

"You didn't even try to at least protect *her?*" With calculation she added, "From…that?"

"Then you heard, I guess." Kate did not respond. Billie Sullivan again gyrated on her chair. "Why? Why should I?"

Kate said bluntly, "Because she's a woman."

"And we have enough trouble without doing it to each other, right? He never wanted to fuck any woman here except her. Never made a move on anybody except her. He heard she liked girls and that turned him on. Explain that one to me."

Kate shrugged. "I can't even begin to understand the way people are about sex."

"He fucked her maybe once every couple weeks, she got a sales manager job out of it. And he didn't do anything else to her, I saw to that, made sure he never saw anything in her but some harmless fluff to fuck once in a while."

"Have you ever been raped?"

"I've been married. Does that count?"

Kate ignored the retort. "I've seen raped women. I would think that another woman—"

"Hey lady copper, there's rape and there's sex you don't want. You don't believe there's a difference? Ever been married? No? Ask married women. Like me, I was, twice. I liked sex but I didn't want the fucking, getting that done to me. All the women I know don't want it either, at least some of the time. The bastards all say they don't know what women want today. We don't want anything more than we ever did. All we are is honest now about the shit they do in bed."

"Not all women feel that way."

"Show me one that doesn't, she's had a lobotomy. Look, lady copper. The boss fucked everybody. If he didn't do it to Gretchen that way he'd have figured out some other way. He fucked everybody some way. Understand?" Her voice was exasperated, as if she were explaining a simple concept to a dull child. "He *had* to do it. It was him, see that? He had to have his brand on everybody's ass." She flicked ash again, pulled at her hair. "I did what I could for her. It was the best I could do. It was *all I* could do."

"Did you never want to change things?"

"Change things," Billie Sullivan repeated.

Kate remained silent; she watched the intake of smoke as Billie Sullivan drew from her cigarette, and the eyes that stared at her in unblinking, unfocused scorn.

"All the Fergus Parkers out there and you want me to change things. What kind of cop are you? This your first case? They had you walking old ladies across the street, right?"

Kate smiled at her. "Who's next?" Surely it would be Harley Burton.

"Maybe...Guy Adams. Not that he could've done it," she added. "I'm talking pure motive here, pure and simple. Guy Adams is a *type.*"

The word had been spoken venomously. "What kind of type?" Kate asked, suspecting that Billie Sullivan's view of Guy Adams was not dissimilar to her own.

"Pretty clothes, pretty face, his mama sent him to one of those Eastern charm schools—"

Kate resisted the impulse to nod, to add that his type also never got mugged or violated, never even conceived of such outrages happening to them. They never even got traffic tickets ...

"Now he looks for women to keep on taking care of him," Billie Sullivan sneered. "Just like my own Daddy does to my Mama. The Ashley Wilkes type, you follow me?"

Kate said, grinning, "The character from *Gone With the Wind* that Scarlett thought was so noble."

"The *wimp* from *Gone With the Wind,*" she corrected her. "A dear old Daddy type. You'd never think I had a Daddy with class, would you? Graduate of Yale? With a daughter who stomped out of Vassar her first year." Screeching with laughter, heedless of the skirt that hiked well above her large-jointed knees, she raised broomstick thin legs encased in red plaid knee socks, and propped transparent plastic sandals on the desk.

"Daddy hasn't talked to me since the day I explained to him what he was doing to Mama and what a world-class asshole he really was. I got more balls than my Daddy and Guy Adams combined. You know how Guy Adams thinks? He thinks he can make phone calls to Philadelphia knocking the boss and get away with it, not have it get back. Guy Adams thinks people like the boss aren't dangerous at all, he thinks they just have bad manners. He doesn't have a *clue.*"

"Do you think any of the people here except you really had a clue about that?"

She contemplated Kate. "Good question, lady copper. I'd say ... maybe. But I'd guess they never compared notes, put it all together. Too embarrassed to admit what they all put up with, all the shit they ate."

"Harley Burton," Kate prodded. "You mentioned before he had the most motive of anybody—if he knew. Knew what?"

"What about me?" she parried. "Aren't you curious why the boss kept me around? Why he liked me?"

"I expect because you understood each other," Kate said drily. "Was there another reason?"

"My source. That's why he really needed me. Milly in Philly. Jonathon Wagner's secretary. He's the president, you know. Me and Milly in Philly are like *that.*" She held up two intertwined fingers. "She was the one that told me about each and every phone call Guy Adams made. Months ago Milly in Philly told me they were reorganizing, the boss was top choice for a big promotion, his region looked so good. That was because the boss's managers were all busting their asses—but anyway, the boss knew six months ago something was breaking and he could plan."

"I see." Kate turned to a fresh page in her notebook.

"No you don't, but you will. Everybody was afraid of the boss except the one guy around here who handles himself. Harley Burton. And he was worse than trouble, he was competition. One more promotion and he'd of been gone, somewhere else in the country, same as the boss in position and title. Who knows from there? Someday the boss might even have to work for a guy who was once under him. Can you imagine that? Then Tampa opened, Harley Burton wanted Pete Webber to get the job, the boss saw his chance. He turned Webber down. Transferred him to new accounts, figuring he might get pissed enough to quit.

Which he did and the boss blamed Harley Burton, demoted him out of that corner office, moved brown-noser Grayson in. And so he had all the talent in his region right under his thumb. Neat?"

"Neat," Kate agreed, making rapid notes.

"There's more. He figured he could walk on Harley Burton—his best man—because Harley Burton wouldn't quit with only a few months left before he had fifteen years in, got vested in the pension plan. Then the boss could move him back into the corner office after the promotion, could afford to then, he'd be two organization levels higher, could always control him. And Harley Burton would see that he had a career again and wouldn't quit. See how cute the boss was?"

"Indeed," Kate said. "What did he plan to do about Fred Grayson?"

She shrugged. "Kick him back down where he came from. Or palm him off on some unsuspecting fool in another region." She grimaced. "The brown-noser came out of this even better than he knows..."

"Did Fergus Parker have plans for anyone else?"

She made a slitting motion across her throat. "That, for Gail Freeman and Guy Adams. If it was the last thing he ever did."

Kate remained silent, diagramming the machinations of Fergus Parker and recording several direct quotes from Billie Sullivan. "Billie," she said, "you didn't place Duane Fletcher anywhere on your list."

"Poor Duane," she said mockingly, "that's what everybody always calls him. Poor Duane. Yeah, the boss kicked his ass all over the office. You know, we sell office furniture here. You'd think Duane was peddling the cure for cancer. Let me tell you about poor Duane. At my house I got cats. Strays come around, two decided to stay. I'd rather have cats than a man anytime, but I'm no Doris Day, I don't even like animals much. Wouldn't have a dog if you paid me. But cats are different. Cats stay because they want to be there. Dogs—you kick a dog and it licks your foot. That's Duane Fletcher."

"You're telling me he didn't have a motive for killing Fergus Parker?"

"Oh shit yes he had a motive," she said impatiently, glaring at Kate, then discarding her butt into the ashtray without bothering to extinguish it. "Don't you catch my drift at all? Not much wonder you cops never catch anybody. What the boss did to Duane, anybody'd want to kill him fifteen times over. But the dog you kick, does it ever kill you? Shit no. Whoever knocked off the boss—you better look for a cat, not a dog like Duane Fletcher."

"I see. So you're telling me Gretchen Phillips and Harley Burton and Gail Freeman are capable."

"Gretchen and Gail Freeman are," she said after a moment. "Some people can take a lot, but only so much ..."

"But not Harley Burton?" She suspected that Billie Sullivan felt an admiration for Harley Burton she would not admit.

"He's capable. More capable than anybody. But I see him walking out the door, saying fuck the pension. I can see him punching the boss's lights out. I don't see—well, Harley Burton wouldn't use a knife, that's all."

"You've been very helpful," Kate said.

"Snitching is what I do best," Billie Sullivan said.

"What'll you do after you leave Modern Office?"

"Go back to work for a while and behave." With a sigh, she removed her feet from the desk. "The typing and dictation shit again. It's been a three-year vacation with the boss. But don't waste any sympathy on me. Milly in Philly laid the word on me a little while ago about the boss's replacement. Would you believe Fred Grayson?"

Kate murmured, "That seems somehow...appropriate."

Again Billie Sullivan bared her teeth in a grin. "I don't figure it'll be long before I find another Fergus Parker and I'll be on vacation again. In the meantime, I have a special farewell in mind when the dink manager comes down here to toss my ass. But don't say anything, okay? Don't spoil my fun."

"There's no reason to say anything. My business is police business."

Kate got up and gave her one of her cards. With a disdainful flip of her wrist, Billie Sullivan tossed it into her cardboard box.

Chapter 17

Ellen had placed her purse in the bottom desk drawer and was sorting through the phone messages for Gail Freeman when her phone rang.

"Ellen, this is Guy. I really need to see you." His voice was low and husky with strain.

"Guy—we just had lunch." *Why me, God? Why this?*

"We didn't get a chance to talk. Can I see you later?"

"Later? You mean—" She broke off; Gail Freeman had strolled by, glanced in, and paused, watching her.

"I'll call you tonight," Guy said. "How about that?"

That would give her time to think of how she could best discourage this man's gentle, if annoying, persistence. "All right," she said, giving Gail Freeman a sign that she would be off the phone quickly. But he waved and sauntered away.

As she walked down the hall from Billie Sullivan's office, Kate glimpsed Guy Adams on his phone, and she realized with pleasure that Ellen would be back from her lunch with the managers. For some minutes longer Kate strolled up and down the hallway, her head down, pondering, assimilating her conversation with Billie Sullivan. Then she went into the lobby.

"Hey Cagney," Judy Markham said softly, smiling, blinking her large blue eyes, "you gonna make a collar soon?"

Kate smiled. "Maybe."

"I always thought it was a joke, people in business stabbing each other. You got an idea who did it?"

"We're working on it," she answered, and walked on, to Gail Freeman's office.

"You can do what you wish now about Billie Sullivan," she told Gail Freeman. "I'm finished interviewing her."

"Good." He pushed a button on his intercom. "Ellen, I'll be in Billie Sullivan's office a few minutes. Don't switch any calls up there."

"Right, Gail."

Ellen, again looking through the phone messages taken by Judy Markham, smiled gladly at the sight of Kate Delafield in her doorway.

"I was wondering," Kate said, "perhaps you'd like to have dinner tonight, give me a chance to—" Repay you, she was going to say, and broke off in irritation at her clumsiness. "Talk to you," she finished. "Give me a chance to show you something besides a browbeating detective." She added in her mind: And a sobbing mess.

"I'd like that, Kate." She thought rapidly, then said, "I absolutely have to stay a little late tonight, I'm so backed up with all that's been going on. Could we get an early sandwich or something?"

"A sandwich would be fine," Kate said, disappointed.

Ellen remembered *The White Cliffs of Dover.* "There's a British pub near here, where I went for lunch." She added with enthusiasm, "I think you might really like it. How about that? Is six-thirty okay?"

"Fine."

"It's over on Washington, it's called—"

"This is Billie Sullivan speaking."

The voice came out of the speaker in the hallway ceiling. "I just had my ass fired from this fucking company and before I go there's a few things I'm gonna tell you suckers."

"Oh dear God," Ellen said, and stood up.

"You're a bunch of dumb assholes, you have to be. You're working here. But I'm gonna give you dumb shits the lowdown on a few things once and for all. None of you peons in word processing could get a two dollar raise last quarter, right? All because of the economy, right? Wrong, assholes. It's because fuckers like Fred Grayson cheat on their expense accounts—"

"Oh holy God," whispered Ellen.

"Indeed," Kate agreed. So this was Billie Sullivan's special farewell.

Ellen rushed from the office, through the lobby toward Billie Sullivan's office, Kate following.

"—Fred Grayson brown bags it every day of his useless life but he puts in expense account vouchers for lunch every day with customers, rips this company off two hundred bucks a week, that's minimum. And so you see, you suckers—"

"Jeez," Judy Markham said, gazing in awe at the ceiling speaker.

"Buzz this door open!" Ellen shouted, tugging at the far lobby door.

"Break this fucking door down!" Fred Grayson screamed, yanking savagely on the knob of Billie Sullivan's closed office door.

"—the fucking over this company's given all you sorry bastards slaving your asses away for peanuts, here's the straight scoop on the last sales meeting of your caring and concerned management in San Francisco. The liquor bill alone—"

"We'd need a battering ram," Gail Freeman said, rapping his

knuckles on the solid door. "Fergus Parker insisted on nothing but the best for his office and hers too."

"—thousand dollars, my dimwitted friends. The food bill alone another five grand, bringing the grand total to a cool eighteen thousand bucks for twenty people to come from the west coast offices and screw around for three days. And I do mean screw around. Furthermore, assholes—"

"God damn it!" screeched Fred Grayson, pounding on the door.

"—nothing's too good for our customers, pretty boy Guy Adams, all he does is come in and sit in his fancy schmancy office and go to lunch, he put in a bill last week, four people at Le Dome, two hundred and forty smackers, you dumb shits—"

"Master key?" Kate suggested.

Several people had emerged from word processing to stare open-mouthed at the group clustered around Billie Sullivan's door. Gretchen Phillips and Harley Burton came around the corner. Guy Adams trotted down the hall.

"Go back to your offices," Gail Freeman called, hands raised in a stop gesture. The word processing people obeyed; Gretchen Phillips, Harley Burton, and Guy Adams did not.

"—fucking lunches could you dumb peons buy for two hundred and forty bucks?"

Gail Freeman said to Kate, "Can you imagine Fergus Parker entrusting me with a key to his office or his secretary's?"

"—and Fred Grayson just put in an expense account for a dinner for five, a modest affair, only a cool six hundred and eighteen—"

Fred Grayson screamed at Kate, "I'm a taxpayer! I *order* you to shoot this goddamned lock off!"

"—long could you dumb shits feed your kids on six hundred and—"

"Mr. Grayson," Kate said, "I don't believe LAPD would consider this police business."

"—beloved senior manager Fred Grayson hates anybody that wears a skirt unless she lets him screw her, hates anybody any color but white. But he's been sniffing after Cassie Franklin's black ass for months—"

"Slander! She's *slandering* me!"

"Then sue her," Kate said.

"—petty cash fund for, you dumb shits? All kinds of interesting activities. Five hundred bucks, that's what Fergus Parker and Fred Grayson offered Cassie Franklin if she and a soul sister would put out for a certain visiting Philadelphia VP named Bob James who likes his ladies black and preferably two at a time—"

Fred Grayson hurled himself at the door, bounced off, grabbed his shoulder.

"Christ," Gretchen Phillips whispered.

Guy Adams stood unmoving, rigid and staring at the door. Harley Burton began to laugh.

"I'll take care of this," Ellen said, and opened the door into the lobby.

"—petty cash fund for panelling Fred Grayson's family room and den and a new golf cart for—" The voice cut off.

Ellen returned, dusting her hands in satisfaction. "The Muzak speaker, I turned it off."

Gail Freeman laughed. "Ingenious, assistant." He leaned up against the wall, grinning. "A solution your high-priced management couldn't come up with. I'll get you a raise one of these days—if we can ever get the company's expenses down."

Gretchen Phillips and Harley Burton laughed. Guy Adams looked bewildered. Fred Grayson stared at Gail Freeman, his eyes stony and filled with malice.

"Black boy, you just watch it there."

"Fred, cut out that crap," growled Harley Burton.

"Hey Fred," Guy Adams said softly, putting a hand on Fred Grayson's arm.

Fred Grayson flung off the arm. "You just watch it you black son—"

"Mr. Grayson that's enough," Kate snapped. "You're in violation of Mr. Freeman's civil rights. You're an officer of this company, in the presence of witnesses you've made a racially derog—"

"What *is* this shit!" Fred Grayson screamed. He turned on Kate. "You *agree* with me!"

"Hardly," Kate said with cold contempt.

"Tell you what, Fred." Gail Freeman's voice was casual; he continued to lean against the wall, hands in his pockets. "Let's settle this outside the office. I'll be quite satisfied beating the living shit out of you."

Ellen glanced in alarm from Gail Freeman's slight frame to the huge bulk of Fred Grayson, and turned to Kate. "You can't let Gail—"

"I can handle myself just fine," Gail Freeman said, his calm dark eyes fixed on Fred Grayson. He flexed his fingers, formed his hands into fists. "And Fred knows it."

Fred Grayson took a rapid step backward. Kate remembered that Gail Freeman had been a boxing champion in the Marines. She did not bother to conceal her grin. "Mr. Grayson, I suggest you apologize."

Gretchen Phillips said, "Fred, what you said is disgusting."

"Show at least a little class, man," Guy Adams said. "If I were Gail—"

"Shut up! Shut up all of you." Not looking at Gail Freeman, Fred Grayson muttered, "It was the heat of the moment. I—"

Billie Sullivan's door edged open; she slipped into the hallway, yellow teeth exposed in a grin, hands held high over her head. "I surrender. Tear me limb from limb."

"Bitch," spat Fred Grayson. "All lies. You bitch, you—"

Kate stepped between them. "Miss Sullivan, perhaps you'd like to be escorted from the building."

"You bet your ass, lady copper." She glided toward Kate.

"We'll send your things," Gail Freeman said. "Kindly exit the premises. Now."

Billie Sullivan linked her arm through Kate's. "I've been thrown out of better places. Come on, lady copper. Take me away from all this shit."

Chapter 18

The phone in the conference room rang; in a throaty voice Judy Markham announced Wesley Miller calling from Philadelphia.

Kate glanced at her watch: three-thirty. "Yes sir," she said cordially. "Working a little late, aren't you?"

"In these hectic economic times we're all working a little harder," Wesley Miller rumbled. "I know you can't discuss the case, but I've just come from an extended meeting with Jonathon Wagner and the executive board about Fergus Parker's successor. Jonathon's asked me to give you a call and see whether you'd at least answer this question. Is Fred Grayson a suspect?"

"Yes sir, he's a suspect."

"Ah, is he just a suspect generally, along with a number of

people? Or is he—as I understand it, your normal procedure is that everyone is under suspicion. Isn't that so?"

Kate decided to parry the question while she considered how she would answer. "Would Mr. Grayson by chance be your choice to succeed Fergus Parker?"

"A manager in Kansas City with a fine record was our first choice. But it's near impossible to find people willing to transfer into your expensive city." Wesley Miller's voice was aggrieved. "Can't say as I blame Bill for turning down the job in these uncertain economic times. He and his wife have a seventy-thousand dollar house in Kansas City they couldn't begin to duplicate in L.A. So we've decided to promote from within. Maybe it's better under these tragic circumstances, give the employees more of a sense of continuity—"

"Isn't Kansas City where Harley Burton came from?" She was searching back through her notes, to her conversation with Fred Grayson.

"Believe it is."

"I understand he's had an outstanding record—"

"Until recently. Can't promote a man who's just been demoted." Wesley Miller's voice had quickened with impatience and annoyance. "And Fred Grayson's our choice. He's senior manager in service, has a record that shows consistency, if not spectacular—"

This isn't police business, Kate thought, shifting the receiver to the other ear as Wesley Miller droned on. Why the hell should she care whom they chose?

But faces drifted through her mind—Harley Burton, Duane Fletcher, Gretchen Phillips—admirable people who had had a Fergus Parker, and now would have a Fred Grayson. And Ellen O'Neil would still be here, would go on working here after this case was closed—if it ever was…

"It's none of my business at all whom you choose, Mr. Miller. And I know you're not interested in other opinions—"

"That's absolutely correct."

Kate kept her voice carefully courteous. "I must say that the choice rather surprises me in view of what I've seen of Mr. Grayson's judgment—"

"Meaning what." Wesley Miller's tone was edgy, hostile.

She chose her first point cautiously. "There's been a public accusation that Mr. Grayson pads his expense account."

Wesley Miller's sigh came clearly over the long distance hum. "Listen, I know I'm talking to a police officer. But I think you know, I think it's public knowledge—well, it's naive to think some expense account padding doesn't go on in every business."

"Yes sir, but two hundred dollars a week seems excessive by any standard."

"*How* much?"

"Two hundred a week. According to Fergus Parker's secretary."

"Oh. Her. Well—"

Kate continued, "And Mr. Grayson's racial prejudice is rather evident."

Wesley Miller spoke slowly, in a tone that seemed bored. "Lots of us feel like we don't want to ah, work with people who get shoved down our throats whether they can do the job or not. With all these damn laws and—"

"Mr. Miller, we don't disagree on that. We talked about it this morning, remember? I feel that way and so do the police officers I work with. I can well understand anyone's feelings on that score." Kate picked up a piece of company stationery from the file folder she had been examining. "What I'm saying is, as an officer of a company with a strongly worded statement on its official stationery promising full commitment to equal opportunity, Mr. Grayson's prejudice is blatant and has become public—"

Wesley Miller interrupted with quiet command, "Blatant in what way?"

He had chosen the first and less important adjective to question; Kate was certain he was now taking notes. She flipped her notebook open to the back page. "Understand, sir, these are not my personal judgments of Mr. Grayson. After eleven years in police work I'm quite accustomed to hearing considerable racial hatred. In my presence Mr. Grayson referred to Mr. Freeman as a nigger, a spook, a coon, a jungle bunny, a spade."

There was lengthy silence. Then Wesley Miller rumbled, "I don't care what a man's personal opinions are so long as he keeps them out of his business life. So long as he's got the damn sense to keep private the things that should be private."

Such wonderful tolerance, Kate thought as she again shifted the receiver.

"Other than to yourself," Wesley Miller said slowly, as if deliberating over his words, "how have these...opinions...of Fred's become public?"

"He called Mr. Freeman 'black boy' before myself, three managers, and one other non-management employee—and would have made another racial slur except that I intervened. It was an ugly and dangerous situation. And I suggest to you that if there is another incident between Mr. Freeman and Mr. Grayson, or if the company ever wishes to take any kind of disciplinary action against Mr. Freeman, this occurrence has made things doubly difficult."

Wesley Miller's breathing was audible, slow and heavy. "Excuse my language, but people find ways to fuck up today I never even heard of when I went into this business." He sighed, an exasperated expulsion of breath. "I'll suggest to Jonathon that we make Grayson acting manager until we can fully discuss this ... development."

"May I make a suggestion, Mr. Miller?" The image of Ellen O'Neil again floated through her mind. She smiled and added, "Purely as an objective outsider."

"Go ahead, can't hurt." Wesley Miller sounded mournful, tired.

"Perhaps you could arrange to come out here for a few days, do your own on-site observing. Mr. Freeman's fired Billie Sullivan, but—"

"Who's Billie Sullivan?"

"Fergus Parker's secretary."

"Oh. Yes. Her."

"She has nothing to gain or lose now, and I suggest you talk with her. Especially about the reasons surrounding Harley Burton's demotion."

"Fergus's reasons for that weren't very convincing... I liked what I saw of Harley Burton. But it was Fergus's bailiwick and he was adamant..." Wesley Miller trailed off.

Taking more notes, Kate guessed. "Mr. Miller, I'll be as candid as I can under the circumstances. Whom we arrest, or when we make an arrest—that's still problematic, we're processing facts. In some cases we know empirically who committed a crime but we can never develop sufficient evidence to prosecute. But the strongest suspects in this case at this moment are all six members of the management staff—the six people who worked directly for or with Fergus Parker."

There was a soft whistle. "That a fact?"

"Yes sir, that's a fact. My point is, Fergus Parker gave a strong enough reason for homicide—for murder, sir—to all six people who worked with him. I think that should tell you something about Fergus Parker, and about this office."

There was a silence. Kate waited, but the silence continued.

"Mr. Miller, it would be good right now psychologically for you to come out here. In these hectic economic times," she said, placing slight emphasis on the phrase, "it seems like a good move for a company's top management to look into things."

After a moment Wesley Miller answered in his resonant voice, "That seems not a half-bad idea. I expect we would probably meet, Detective Delafield."

Kate smiled. "I expect we probably would."

"We're always on the lookout, you know, for smart capable wo—people who show confidence and good judgment, handle themselves well, these are rare commodities, you know. We can always find places in our organization for...people like you."

Caught off-guard, Kate was pleased. "I thank you for the high compliment, Mr. Miller. But my field is law enforcement."

"And I think you should stay in law enforcement. We're a big organization, Detective Delafield. With various needs for that kind of expertise. I don't know how well they're treating you where you are, but you could listen and see if we might not be able to treat you a little better. Never hurts to talk, I always say. Never hurts to listen."

"No sir, indeed it doesn't." Kate sat back in her chair,

smiling, looking out over the hazy sun-splashed city. "It's nice out here right now. Santa Ana winds off the desert are expected for the next few days. You bring your swim trunks when you come."

Chapter 19

The White Cliffs of Dover seemed dimmer at night, the buzz of conversation livelier, friendlier. The patrons, mostly men, were more casually dressed than at lunch—windbreakers and work pants, jeans and sweaters. Two plump middle-aged women, lumpy in woolen skirts and sweaters, were at one of the dart boards; they emitted smothered explosions of giggles as they launched high-arched darts.

Ellen smiled at Kate. "Guy says Modern Office people come here all the time for lunch. To relax, play darts. I can see why—it's so comfortable and homey."

"Harley Burton invited me for your lunch today." Kate drank her ale with enjoyment, amused by the women at the dart board. "I was sorry I couldn't come. I do like it here." She watched the two women return to their table. A mustachioed man in a navy blue cotton jacket made a mocking gesture toward the dart board; one of the women fondled his graying hair and then patted it back into place. Married, Kate thought; you can always tell.

She returned her attention to Ellen, pleased again by the simplicity of her clothes: the severely tailored dark green jacket, short and without collar or lapels; the matching skirt and pale green blouse tied at the throat by a thin dark green ribbon. Her gaze lingered on Ellen's throat, drifted down to her breasts. Memory of the feeling and taste of her was interrupted by the shifting of Ellen's body as she raised her beer mug. Kate looked at her hands: ringless. She remembered the apartment where Ellen lived with Stephanie Hale. Not Westwood or Beverly Hills, but a very good section on the westside. And well-furnished, spacious.

"Have you never wanted to own a house, Ellen? Rent on your apartment must be fairly close to a house payment."

"I would love to own a house," Ellen said fervently. "I'd give *anything* to have a place to call my own. I *hate* paying rent. You might as well throw all that money out onto the street. But Stephie—she thinks it's too obvious, two women owning a house together."

"Why should she care? She's tenured, isn't she?"

"She still doesn't want anyone to know."

I hate this Stephanie Hale. "She's deluding herself," Kate said shortly. "People know. If we really think people don't know, we're just kidding ourselves. Straight people with half a brain pick up all the signs. Not how we act, but how we don't act— how we don't fit in with all the heterosexual game playing. We put on an act and they all laugh behind our backs. You know it happens, Ellen, you've heard the straight people laugh at us. The men especially. When you're not interested in them they're only too happy to sneer and call you queer."

Ellen asked, "They know then … about you?"

Kate chuckled bitterly. "I've never pretended to be heterosexual. But I've never made any announcements either, and never will. Why give anyone a weapon? And it *is* a weapon. I'll give you one possible scenario: Avowed lesbian denies accusation of making sexual advance to female prisoner."

"Kate...could that really happen? I mean—"

"Yes, Ellen, it could happen. And yes, I'm paranoid. But with good reason. And yes they know about me—without my telling them, and they're much happier that way. The brass loves me because I don't call in with problems about my kids, I don't take maternity leave. And the men love me because they're convinced any woman who wants to be a cop must be suffering from penis envy and my being a lesbian confirms that. And the men can tell their wives, 'Yeah, honey, I'm working with a woman but not to worry because she's a lez.' And so the men's wives love me too. So I'm the perfect woman cop. Everyone can respect my work but still be contemptuous. So women can do the job, they tell themselves, but only because they're pseudo-men. But gay male cops can't do the job at all—and they'll prove *that* if they have to kill them to do it."

"You can't mean that," Ellen said in an appalled whisper.

"Yes, I do mean it. I'm not nearly as bad off as the men, Ellen. All gay male cops are in the deepest darkest end of the closet. You think there's resistance to women? Think about the fact that being a cop is one of the big macho trips of the western world, the cop is today's cowboy. They *pay* you to wear that uniform, all that leather, that gun on your hip. They *pay* you to control and intimidate. Ever ask yourself why anyone would *want* to be a cop? The psychological tests screen out many pathological types, but there's still a whole masculine self-image built up around being a cop."

Kate stared into her beer mug, rotating it in her hands. Then she spoke with the firm swiftness of utter conviction. "All the straight cops I know hate the idea of gay male cops with a rage that's simply indescribable. How dare any faggot invade their macho world and think he can be brave and strong and tough? The gay men out on the lines are all in the closet, Ellen, they have to be. You're a gay man in a dangerous situation and all that has to happen is your partner doesn't do what he's supposed to do quite soon enough, the backup you've called for doesn't get there quite soon enough. And you're one dead gay cop who just wasn't *man* enough to be a cop."

Kate looked up to see Ellen staring at her with stricken eyes. "Straight cops...would do that? They're all...like that?"

"Not all. But enough."

"Then why do you stay? Why did *you* want to be a cop?"

Kate spoke more slowly, remembering, and gathering her thoughts. "After Vietnam, after all I'd seen over there, I felt serious about people, Ellen. I wanted to ... help. I joined LAPD in 'seventy-two and worked in juvenile, that's where most women in law enforcement worked then, it was all we could expect. Then the courts mandated numbers, which was the only way I'd have ever gotten into the more challenging areas of police work. I became fascinated by what I saw, the raw edge of lives I could never imagine. People different from me, and other people just like me, but caught in crosscurrents that turned their lives in directions they never conceived of. All our lives are under thread-thin control that can snap so easily—by something as simple as an oil tanker jackknifing on a freeway." It was the first time she had freely spoken of Anne's death, and she was astonished at the calmness of her voice.

Ellen said earnestly, "But you're so *good* at what you do. What you do is so *important.*"

Kate shook her head. "I don't feel that way anymore. For too long I've made the common mistake of all gay people. Believed if I was good enough, being gay wouldn't matter. Well, being good doesn't matter, makes no difference at all. Nothing I do makes any real difference to anybody."

"That's not true, Kate," Ellen said softly, "that's just not true. I think you're just tired...and maybe it's time for you to think about getting out of it. Maybe it's time to do other things you're good at."

Kate was silent, thinking of Gretchen Phillips. *I'm one of the few women,* Gretchen Phillips had said, *who could afford to pay Fergus Parker's price for my job.*

Kate looked down at the hands curved around her beer mug. *I paid that price too—because of Anne. I no longer have to pay any price for any job.*

"You're right," she said, smiling at Ellen and raising her beer mug in a toast. "I don't even have to care about the mortgage anymore." She took a deep draught of her beer, feeling suddenly light and free. She thought of Wesley Miller, of his promise of other opportunities.

Ellen said in alarm, "You will give it a lot of thought, won't you, Kate? You need to get a good perspective on things before you do anything. After all the years you've given to your work, it's too important a decision."

"I will. And you should give a lot of thought to your own life. None of us should surrender our dreams to other people. Anne's dream was to finish college, get her degree. Anne thought a college degree would confer some magical mark on her." Kate smiled, remembering; then she looked directly into Ellen's eyes. "I was the selfish one in our relationship. I kept telling her next year—she had plenty of time. You're thirty-one. Anne was thirty-two when she died."

Their food arrived; gratefully, Ellen attended to salting her french fries, tasting her fish. But the somberness of Kate's face continued to disturb her. "Billie Sullivan," she said lightly, "that was quite an exit." She was gratified when Kate chuckled.

"I've never met anyone remotely like her."

Ellen asked carefully, "The case, can you tell me anything about it, how it's coming?"

"Well, a pattern's begun to emerge—as it always does in any case of homicide that isn't random violence." She took a bite of her fish. "Haven't you been upset enough by all this, Ellen?"

"I might be useful," she answered quickly. "Even as a sounding board. I'm getting to know some of these people now. If you feel you can trust me."

"It isn't a question of trust—" She broke off. Of course it was. Hadn't she always told Anne about the cases she was working on? With judicious editing of the grosser detail, of course. How could she not trust Ellen O'Neil?

"There are some problems." She buttered a piece of hot crusty bread. "We're still sifting through fingerprint evidence— it's still the most conclusive proof we can have in a criminal case." She decided she would not mention Harley Burton's partial print on the coffee pot. "We have a cigarette butt we picked up on the fifteenth floor, the lab's lifted an unusual blood type from the saliva. The butt's of very limited value but I'm certain the killer discarded it in his haste."

"Why limited value? I'd think it would be an important piece of evidence."

"It's presumptive evidence. A defense attorney would argue the butt could be anybody's—anyone from any floor in that building could've dropped it. When we make an arrest we'll use it of course if we can match up the blood type—it's unusual enough to be useful. And everything adds weight to a circumstantial case." She ate a piece of bread. "You never find really good bread like this anymore."

"Kate, do you know who did it?"

Kate watched two young men begin to throw darts, flinging them with easy expertise; then she looked into light brown eyes wide with concern, and decided to speak the truth.

"The evidence points to four management people, Ellen. From your signed statement, the statements of the two guards, we know within a few seconds the elapsed time from the moment of the killing, we know the essential fact that it took the killer less than two minutes to get all the way down those stairs and mingle with arriving employees. On that basis, I've eliminated as suspects Gretchen Phillips and Duane Fletcher."

She said in dismay, "And included my boss—the one person I admire most."

Of the four, Kate reflected, Harley Burton was the man she herself admired most. "Unless something unexpected develops, it would appear to be one of them—from the standpoint of opportunity. But when it comes to criminality, there still has to be motive, malice, intent. I'll concede," she said grudgingly, "that Guy Adams seems the least likely from a motive standpoint."

"I knew it, I just *knew* that," Ellen said triumphantly.

"He's still a strong suspect, Ellen," Kate warned. "There are other problems, inconsistencies. The medical examiner says that blood spurted onto the killer's hand or sleeve. Gail Freeman and Fred Grayson wore dark suits that day, but light shirt cuffs. And Guy Adams wore a cream-colored jacket. But what do you do about bloodstains when you've got only a scant few minutes before police are all over the scene? I'm sorry," she said as Ellen put down her fork. "This isn't appropriate dinner conversation."

"It's not that, it's all right ... I was just thinking..." She said slowly, unwillingly, "Harley Burton doesn't wear a jacket in the office. And he rolls up his sleeves."

Kate nodded, pleased with her. "Yes, I noticed that. And that makes Harley Burton a very strong suspect indeed. But there's still a problem—"

A shout went up from the dartboard; Kate looked over to see three darts crowded into the bullseye. "Nice shooting," she said. "There's the one element that just doesn't make sense, Ellen. No sign of struggle. How could Fergus Parker let Harley Burton or anyone else come at him with a knife? It doesn't make sense. How could he just *allow* himself to be stabbed?"

She ate a french fry, thinking that she would not describe to Ellen the unusual nature of the stab wound. There was another shout from the dart board; she glanced over and then sat utterly motionless, staring at the dart that had thudded into the bullseye and still quivered from the impact. In dawning comprehension she turned and met Ellen's eyes, wide with shock and staring into hers.

"He threw it," Ellen whispered.

"Yes. Of course. Exactly." Kate put down her fork and looked again at the dart board and said wonderingly, "That's just not done. It's not. Not in this day and age. Except in Kung Fu movies...and the odds against a fatal wound... I've never even heard of a case..."

She stared down at her dinner knife, sorting through and fitting images together. A well-crafted, well-balanced knife could be thrown with deadly effect—especially by someone who was accustomed to throwing objects—like darts—with accuracy. And if thrown with velocity... A knife striking Fergus Parker squarely and with force...causing him to fall heavily backward...

Ellen's mind was filled with images of Gail Freeman, Guy Adams, Fred Grayson, and Harley Burton at lunch, at the dart board. It couldn't be Gail—not the way he threw his darts, the delicate flip from behind his ear. And not with that ironic toast at lunch; he could never have killed and then made a boastful toast...But Guy, the way he threw his darts—swiftly, with skill and confidence... But dammit, Kate Delafield could talk for a hundred years about meek little men who were monsters, Guy Adams was not *capable*. Then she remembered Fred Grayson sighting along his darts as if they were weapons ... the powerful thuds of Harley Burton's darts into his target. She shuddered, and glanced at Kate; she was picking at her food, eyes distant with thought. It might very well be Harley Burton. Too bad. It was simply too bad anyone had to be punished for killing a creature like Fergus Parker—Fergus Parker was the monster, not his killer.

Kate ate automatically, her mind absorbed. "I'm sorry," she said, suddenly realizing that considerable time had elapsed.

"I understand perfectly," Ellen told her, smiling.

Kate absently buttered another piece of bread. "I just need to go over my notes, all the details again. And look at the facts—" She looked at the knife, touched her forefinger and thumb lightly to the butter on the blade, held the knife in a clean area as if to throw it; then she inserted the knife into her bread and drew it out, staring at the smeared glossy surface.

"I won't keep you much longer," Ellen teased, watching the fine lines of concentration again deepen between the light blue eyes.

Kate glanced at her watch. "And vice versa. I'll let you get home."

"Kate, if you find out something important from all this ... Will you call me later?"

"Of course. I'd be glad to." She added, "To know if you feel ...okay. Safe." She should be careful, not have Ellen think she was moving in on the UCLA professor's territory—even if she was.

After Ellen left, Kate displayed her shield to a bartender in shirt and pants of matching red plaid, who gave her permission to use the phone on the bar. She called Joe D'Amico at the lab, covering one ear; noise had increased with the progression of the evening.

"I hear from the background the big butch cop is out there risking life and limb," D'Amico growled.

Kate grinned; obviously D'Amico was alone in the lab. She jammed the receiver to her ear as a chorus of moans and boos went up from the crowd around the pool table. "Joe you sweet thing, do me a favor? I'll buy you a lovely new apron for Christmas." D'Amico, a burly and snarling presence in his lab, was a gourmet cook who created dishes of lightness and delicacy, a reflection of his true nature.

"How can I resist, dear heart? I'm so tired of the twelve aprons I have. What do you want?"

She cupped a hand around the mouthpiece of the receiver as the noise level rose again. "The guy yesterday, obese, about five-nine—"

"Parker, yeah. Lardass. Took up two slabs."

D'Amico's voice had dropped into its usual gruff toughness; someone had come into his lab.

"The very one. I need a test on the weapon. I need it now."

There was a burst of cheering and applause; a ragged chorus of *For He's a Jolly Good Fellow* rose from the pool table. Kate ground the receiver into her ear. "What, Joe? Can't hear you!"

"—fucking kind of test do you want?"

"Screening for any foreign material present," Kate shouted.

"—set up a chromatography—"

Kate shouted, "I'll be at the station in half an hour! That okay?"

"—fucking thing as soon as I can and no sooner." D'Amico hung up.

Kate glanced at her watch. Eight-ten. She was only minutes away from the station. She settled herself at the bar, happy in the realization that no one in this place had taken the slightest note of her presence. She ran a hand pleasurably over the rough-grained wood of the bar, signaled for another ale, and relaxed and watched the dart games, listening to the buzz and shout of conversation, allowing warmth and conviviality to flow over her.

Chapter 20

Ellen stopped at a supermarket and picked up a six-pack of Michelob. Then, after she had gone through the checkout line, she returned and defiantly chose a bottle of chilled Johannesburg Reisling. It wouldn't kill her to have a relaxing glass or two before bedtime this once. A gift, she would tell Stephanie. From a Modern Office customer.

The phone was ringing as she unlocked the apartment.

"Darling? Is everything okay?"

"Everything's fine, Stephie. I just—"

"I've been calling since *six.*"

"I worked overtime." Oh screw it, she thought. "Then had dinner with a friend."

"Which friend?"

"Are you checking on me?"

"Are you stepping out?" The tone was facetious.

"Do you think I am?"

"I wouldn't be surprised."

As usual, Stephanie was being cynical and self-pitying. Ellen said nastily, "Are you sure you aren't really just tired of you and me?"

"Let's drop this, Ellen. We should never try to talk about anything serious over the phone. Is everything all right? Are they any closer to arresting someone? There was even an item in the papers here."

"I think they're very close." She was suddenly exhausted; she didn't feel like talking to Stephanie, or doing anything at all. "How's the conference coming?"

"Terrific. And here's the big news, baby. Phillips wants me to come up with another book proposal, expanding on what we did before. Isn't that wonderful?" Stephanie's voice quickened with animation. "How'd you like to quit that job in a few more months and help out again?"

"We'll discuss it," Ellen said after a moment.

"Such enthusiasm." She added, "Another *book*, Ellen darling. It means I'll get my full professorship—"

"I'm tired, Stephie. These last two days have been such a strain... And didn't you just say we shouldn't talk about anything serious on the phone? Isn't a major commitment of my time serious?"

"You're right. Darling, of course you're absolutely right."

She was being unusually docile, Ellen thought.

"And don't bother about picking me up," Stephanie said. "Jim's wife will drop us both off." She added, "She doesn't work."

Irritated by the subtle pressure, Ellen said, "Tell me how the sessions went."

She walked over to the television, dragging the phone cord, switched on the set. She sat heavily in an armchair and curled her legs up under her and listened, eyelids drooping with tiredness, to the cadence of Stephanie's voice.

After a final "I love you too," she hung up, and disinterestedly opened the *Herald Examiner*. She preferred the *Times*, but Stephanie liked the *Herald's* sports page.

MID WILSHIRE GRAY FLANNEL MURDER
The bold two-column headline leaped at her from page three. A smaller subheading read, OFFICE DESIGN EXEC SLAIN.

Fergus Parker, 48, top ranking west coast executive of Modern Office, Inc. was a victim of stabbing early yesterday.

The body was discovered by Ellen R. O'Neil, 31, an employee, shortly before the highrise suite of offices opened for the day.

Robbery was not an apparent motive, according to Lt. James R. Kovich, who also

The shrill of the phone startled her. Could it be Kate? So soon? She folded the paper before picking up the receiver.

"I've been calling and calling," her mother said. "First you don't answer and I picture you lying there in a pool of blood, the Gray Flannel Murderer has got in there and got you. And then the phone is busy and I'm so relieved, and then it's busy and busy and I'm picturing you calling for help and the Gray Flannel Murderer is strangling you and the phone is dangling off the—"

Laughing, Ellen said, "Mother, you're crazy."

"Did you see the *Herald?* Mrs. Fox next door showed me. The *Times* is too refined to have such a writeup. Gray Flannel Murder," her mother snorted. "And they even put your age in the paper—"

"I don't care at all."

"You will. I give you five more years and you'll start forgetting a birthday or two."

"Maybe," Ellen said wearily. She glanced at the wall clock: eight forty-five.

"Ellen sweetheart, are you all right?"

"Sure, Mother. Just tired."

"You sure that's all? Your tough and capable detective, is she ever going to catch anybody?"

"Any time now. I'm really tired, Mother. I think I'll just go to bed and curl up with some nice poetry."

"You sure you're—"

"Don't worry, Mother," she said firmly, "the Gray Flannel Murderer hasn't the slightest interest in me. Good night, I'll call you tomorrow."

She got up and threw the *Herald Examiner* in the trash, and walked into the bedroom. "God damn it," she muttered, glaring at the jumbled bedclothes, the rumpled blue pajamas. There was no way to explain those pajamas, she'd better wash them. And the sheets, too. She changed into her usual jeans and shirt and tennis shoes, and put fresh sheets on the bed.

As she was returning to her apartment from the laundry room she glimpsed, to her surprise and displeasure, Guy Adams in the hallway, talking with her next-apartment neighbors, Carl and John.

Guy walked quickly to her and in a gesture as naturally affectionate as if she were his sister, placed his hands on her shoulders and touched a smooth-shaven cheek to her face. She was disarmed by his gentleness. His faint scent was of woods and autumn, too delicate for cologne; expensive shaving lotion, she guessed.

"I tried to call you earlier. I was out to dinner—I just came on over. Your friends here were nice enough to let me in."

I'm sure they were, she thought. Their glances lingered covetously on Guy Adams, slender and elegant in a white velour turtleneck and dark brown slacks.

"Let me talk to you, Ellen. Just a few minutes."

He looked tired and dispirited, forlorn as a child. Touched, she impulsively took his hand and led him to her apartment.

He sat on the sofa, his body stiffly erect, his hand still clutching hers.

"Guy, you're so tense."

"This is a nightmare."

She knew she could not so much as hint at Kate's confidences, and she answered softly, "Of course. Would you like something to drink? We don't have liquor, I'm sorry. But there's beer, and I have a very nice bottle of wine, Stonegate—"

He said abruptly, "Beer's fine."

"I can give you some grass if you'd prefer. Very good stuff.

Guaranteed by the UCLA student body and faculty," she added drily.

"Smoking grass'll make me want cigarettes. Dumb as it seems, I'm really trying to quit. Beer's fine."

In the kitchen, as she opened two Michelobs and poured them into glasses, her impulse of generosity toward Guy Adams evaporated. He would not be much of a problem to get rid of, she'd just ease him out as quickly as possible . She came back to find him morosely gazing at the television screen, his hands repeatedly smoothing the sharp creases in his slacks.

"You can't stay long," she said, and added, hating herself, "My boyfriend will be home soon. He—he's very jealous."

He nodded without looking at her and took a glass from her hand and drank half its contents before setting it down on the table. "Thank you, Ellen. That's good." He took a deep breath. "I'm going absolutely crazy."

She sat down next to him on the sofa.

Taylor sat at his desk in a bright wash of light, finishing reports and cleaning up paperwork. He got up and pursued Kate to her desk.

Her phone was ringing, and he placed a hand over the receiver to prevent her picking it up. "I got big news, Kate."

"Me too, Ed. Our killer threw the knife."

Taylor's eyes widened, then clouded as he made mental connections. "Yeah...yeah...Jesus, weird. Simple. Logical. I never thought...Jesus, this business can make you feel like a damn moron. Paydirt on the wine bottle. Just came in."

Her phone had stopped ringing. Taylor fished in a pocket of his jacket, produced a scrap of paper. He read laboriously, "Robert Mondavi Cabernet Sauvignon ... A seal Baker found in all that glass fit the neck of that bottle perfectly."

Kate's phone rang again. "Prints?" She picked up the receiver.

"Prints?" Taylor repeated rhetorically. His eyes gleamed with satisfaction. "To begin with, latents from Fergus Parker—"

"Kate?" It was Joe D'Amico. "There were microscopic traces in the grooves of the knife handle, traces of undissolved material in the blood sample we wiped from the knife. Chemical analysis shows an organic compound composed of the following—" D'Amico's voice was flat; he was reading. "Phosphorous, sulphur, hydrogen sulphide—"

"Joe," Kate said, "give it to me in English." She sat tensely; the warmth and conviviality of *The White Cliffs of Dover* had evaporated in the harsh reality of the station and D'Amico's impartial voice.

"Oil, Kate. Some kind of petroleum product."

Kate said automatically, "Joe, I owe you." She hung up and turned to Taylor.

"Also on the seal and wine bottle," Taylor gloated, "were clear and perfect prints of fingers contaminated with foreign matter—"

"The lab just gave me the same answer. Found oil traces on the knife, in the blood on the knife. He opened the hood of his car, Ed. Unscrewed his radiator cap—that's where he picked it up on his fingers."

"Yup. You bet we're gonna find matching samples on the handkerchief Hansen collected from his car."

Kate said in consternation, "I asked Joe to run that test thinking it would help clear him."

"Amateur City, you can never tell. But I never figured Guy Adams."

Kate did not answer.

"We'll pick him up," Taylor said.

Guy Adams said, "It's amazing how fast you understood what kind of man Fergus Parker was. It took me up until yesterday to really know. Thank God you understood. Women have been the best people ever to happen to me in my life. Ellen," he said miserably, "I need you to understand why it happened, how it happened. We share a bond now, Ellen. I owe it to you. *I need* you to know."

Ellen had just begun to lift her beer glass. She dropped it

down onto the coffee table where it teetered, rattled, wobbled, righted itself.

His voice was a faint whisper. "I still can't believe it happened."

His eyes were fixed on the television screen, and Ellen glanced over thinking she must have misunderstood, that something on television would surely explain what he had just said. They sat in silence, watching two cops pursue a man down an alley.

He said, "Why have you been avoiding me?"

Out of her numbed mind came a clear warning: *Careful. Just be careful.*

"I wasn't avoiding you, Guy."

"Didn't you know—couldn't you imagine how I felt?"

"I—maybe...who can—" she stuttered, "maybe no one can know that, know—"

"You're upset. Don't be upset." His voice rose. "Why are you upset?"

Be careful. Be very very careful. "I'm fine Guy. I just...feel bad. For you."

"I hardly ever got there early, Ellen. Just once before so early. But it was a report, a survey they needed in Philadelphia, I just had to get it finished ... I knew he was in. From my office I could hear him shouting and laughing, that awful bray of his. But I figured he wouldn't know I was in. I made coffee—"

She started as the phone rang.

"God," he said. "Not now. Just ignore it."

After five rings he got up. "I'll just unplug it."

"Wait," she said through a dry throat. She got up. "Mother—it's my mother, Guy. She said she'd call now—she's only a few blocks away, if I don't answer she'll come over to ... see why."

He stared at her.

"I'll just tell her I'll call her back, that's all." She walked over to the phone as he did not reply. *Let it be Kate...*She picked up the receiver.

"Ellen? Ellen it's—"

"Mother, I've got company." The quaver in her voice caught in her throat, and she coughed to clear it. "I'll call you later."

She hung up. She walked back to the man staring at her from the sofa.

Kate looked at the phone in her hand. Guy Adams was with Ellen. If he knew Ellen had tried to protect him ... If Ellen had told him...

He thinks she saw him!

She slammed the phone down.

Taylor called from his desk, "Kate, what—"

Kate came from behind her desk, running.

"I'd just gotten more coffee and was walking into my office as he came out of the executive washroom. 'Leave that coffee and come to my office, boy,' he calls to me. 'I got a job for you.' Like I was a two-year old. I had no idea ... I went back with him. Harley's talked to me about sales, something I'd really like to get into and—" Guy raised a hand in a gesture of futility, dismissal. "He sat down in his big chair—God, it's indelible, all this. He told me not to sit down, to open a bottle of wine, he couldn't manage his corkscrew. He's sitting there, a foot on his desk, his hands behind his head, grinning like ... like ..."

He rubbed his palms back and forth on his dark brown slacks. "I thought there was still a possibility we could talk ... I went to the cart, he told me to roll it over. He couldn't be bothered getting up. I was his serf. I told him I didn't know what was going on—I'd had enough. He could open his own bottle. And he said, 'You want to work for this company one minute after March thirty-first, boy, you better damn well move that cart over here.'"

He took a deep breath and looked at her. She looked back steadily, scarcely breathing. His face had a greenish pallor against the white pullover, his eyes were fevered.

"Amateur City!" Kate shouted at Taylor as they roared down Pico leading a caravan of two other flashing police cars. A motorcycle thundered out from a side street to join them. "With an amateur cop who couldn't see past her own nose! If he does anything to her—goddammit!" She swerved around a panel truck.

"Slow down, Kate!" shouted Taylor, clutching the dashboard.

She grated, "Adams was so sick he was *green*. Like a damn fool I listened to my instincts instead of my training. *I assumed* he was in shock! If I'd flat out *asked* if he'd done it, he'd have caved like cardboard!"

Kate hit the brake as she came up behind two cars traveling abreast. Savagely, she pounded the horn. The car in the right lane speeded up and she gunned around the car on the left as it began to pull over—its driver a tiny old man who peered over at her with terrified eyes—and she barely avoided a sideswipe.

"Shit, Kate!" Taylor screamed, again clutching the dashboard.

"So I pulled the cart over. It was heavy, rickety, all those liquor bottles clinking together. Then he wanted to know which of the wines was best. There was a bottle of Robert Mon—I'm rambling."

He took another deep breath. "I had trouble breaking the seal. He slid that big ugly letter opener of his across the desk. He told me I should at least be capable of opening wine. Never, he'd never talked to me like that. I just looked at him. He said to finish, he'd explain. By then I knew what it was—a huge step up the ladder for this hideous man. He poured himself a glass—drank a toast. To himself—the new director of company operations west of the Mississippi. He drank that wonderful wine down like it was his disgusting soda pop. Then he told me for being such a good boy he'd explain how piss-poor my future with the company would be."

He paused, his shoulders heaving. "The company...I'm so proud...my family... My job, Ellen, it's my whole life. It was like ...like I was...it was inconceivable, a nightmare." He picked up his beer and drained it, looked at her. "Could I have more?"

The police caravan was strung out, seconds behind them; and there would be other units at Ellen O'Neil's apartment building probably by now.

"Ed," Kate shouted, "he said he couldn't remember if his damn door was open yesterday, but he *must* have remembered to close it Monday night, Gail Freeman had just *reminded* him, it stands to *reason*—"

"He give you anything in the interview?" Taylor sat back as they sped down a brief stretch clear of traffic.

"Didn't say much at all, my fault. I did a lousy interview, he never really answered my questions, I never gave him a chance to cave, he never tried to justify himself like everybody does, it was all there if I'd just seen it. But I didn't read him right because I *hated* the son of a bitch!"

As Kate weaved through another string of cars she snatched a hand from the steering wheel to clap it to her head. "Sick! Adams was *sick!* He threw a knife into Fergus Parker and ran downstairs—that cretin in the garage, it wasn't somebody coughing—it was Guy Adams throwing up!"

"Maybe the woman's okay, Kate. He's such a piece of dogfood maybe he's not capable—"

"I already made that mistake, Ed. Even a weasel protects itself when it's in a corner—goddammit!" She swerved around a Toyota truck pulling out from a curb, fought the wheel.

"Kate! You goddamn idiot slow down!"

Kate righted the car, stamped the accelerator. The car leapt forward.

Ellen went into the kitchen and poured another Michelob, straining for the sound of sirens. But they wouldn't come with sirens, she realized. That would panic him and ...I'm probably wrong, she thought, God knows I've been wrong about everything else so far, but he won't hurt me—if I just don't do anything, say anything... He's on the edge, right on the edge...

She returned to the living room with his beer, sat beside him.

He drank, and clutched his beer glass in a white-knuckled hand. "He told me what he'd done to people. Gretchen—oh God, poor Gretchen. Gail was as good as finished, he'd see to that. I was dead in the company—he knew all about my phone calls to Philadelphia. I'd end up in a nowhere office so small I'd be lucky to have a desk let alone a telephone."

He picked up the remote control, clicked off the television. "I walked to the door. He stood up and said, 'Where you going, boy? You stealing my letter opener, boy? You gutless little fag?' Called me a *fag*." His voice broke. He coughed, swallowed audibly. "I'd put his letter opener in my pocket... He started to laugh, and laugh and laugh... And he said, 'I got you right by your so-called balls, you little fag.' "

His breathing was rapid, ragged. "He was standing there—a howling puffed up creature from hell—nothing God could ever mean to have on this earth...Ellen, you'd throw a stone at a snake or a rat...wouldn't you? I threw what I had in my hand. I threw it..."

He got up, and carrying his beer glass, began to pace. "Blood, there was blood. He fell back into his chair. I was...I was...His eyes bulged out... He pointed to me... Tried to say something... Grabbed at his chest... Blood on his hands... Red, all red..."

Ellen buried her face in her hands. It was worse than Kate Delafield had described, unimaginably worse...

Kate's car screeched to a stop; she shouted to Taylor, "Pull in the driveway! Quick!" She leaped from the car as a squad car and then another pulled up behind them. Kate signalled for two men to cover the rear of the building, the others to enter.

"Ellen, I had to tell you—tell somebody."

She looked at him out of tear-blurred eyes. "I know you did, Guy. It's all right."

"My mind—jelly. I ran into the hall, you were there with the coffee pot...looking for me. And then there was this sound... this awful sound from his office, from him. And I started to throw up. I ran, just ran, trying to hold it down, to get away from him, all the way down those stairs, my stomach heaving and heaving, all the way down...through the garage...to my car ... Threw up everything in me...Then the police were arriving. I just waited to be arrested."

He ceased pacing, turned and looked at her. "I didn't understand what was happening till you said you didn't tell anybody my door was open. Then I knew you'd seen me—you were protecting me. Still I thought I'd be arrested, the police would find proof, I thought you'd change your mind. Every cop that came up to me, I thought I'd be arrested, especially that woman detective...But nothing's happened."

He stood very still, looking at her. "You're the only one who knows."

Kate raced ahead of the car, held up a hand, jumped onto the hood and then the roof. She braced, then leaped for Ellen's balcony wall, grasped the top, and dangled until she could get leverage for her feet, cursing the smooth soles of her shoes. She pulled herself up and over, onto the balcony.

"All last night I had nightmares. What if they arrest somebody else? Gretchen. Or Gail. And if I got away with it there'd be a cloud over everybody in that office forever—"

"Give yourself up, Guy." She spoke softly, firmly. "Explain what happened."

"I don't know what they'd—what they'd do to me."

"There are extenuating circumstances." She was calm; she knew her voice had the conviction of utter rightness. "Guy, tell them exactly what you've told me. Exactly. What happened to Fergus Parker you didn't mean to happen, everybody who's ever known you can testify to that. And everybody knew what he was like. What could be worse than what you've been going through?"

He walked toward her. "You see why I needed to talk. Why—"

Through the gauzy curtain Kate saw Guy Adams go toward Ellen with an object in his hand. She seized the small wooden table on the balcony, swung with all her strength.

Ellen screamed as the balcony door exploded in a shower of glass, as Kate Delafield burst into the room and crouched, the gun in her two hands trained on Guy Adams.

"Right there, right there or you're dead."

"Holy God," Guy Adams said, stopping in mid-stride.

The object in Guy Adams' hand, Kate saw, was a beer glass. Ellen ran to her; Kate shifted the gun to one hand and pushed Ellen behind her.

"I'm all right, Kate."

"Stay behind me," Kate ordered.

"I'm fine. He wasn't going to hurt me."

Taylor, gun in hand, breathing loudly, stepped through the shattered balcony door and straightened his jacket and tie. "Jesus Christ you're trying to kill me, Kate." He picked his way through the glass. "Running down sixteen flights of stairs, jumping onto balconies—"

Kate grinned; under stress, Taylor as usual was trying to be funny.

"Lay off me," Taylor said. "I promise never to tell you

another joke." He turned to Ellen. "Miss O'Neil, I'm glad you're okay." He holstered his gun and approached Guy Adams. "You want to do Miranda, Kate? Or should I do the honors?"

"Guy Adams," Kate said, "you're under arrest and will be charged with homicide. You have the right to remain silent, anything you say can and will be used against you in a court of law. You have the right—"

Guy Adams began to cry; tears streamed swiftly down his face. Wrenched with pity, Ellen moved toward him, but Kate held her back.

"Kate, it's all right—"

Kate did not relax her grip. "In a minute." She finished reciting Guy Adams' rights to him and asked repeatedly did he understand until he finally responded yes in a voice of misery. She nodded to Taylor.

"Police!" came a shout from the hallway.

Taylor opened the door. Half a dozen blue-uniformed cops milled about the room as Taylor patted his hands routinely down Guy Adams' body. Kate released Ellen only when Guy Adams, still sobbing, was handcuffed.

Ellen went to him, smoothed the tears from his face. "Guy, it'll be okay," she whispered. "Believe me, it'll be okay."

"Will you come with me now…down there? Stay with me?"

"Of course I will."

"Put him in the car, Ed," Kate said. "We'll be right along."

"Ellen?"

"I'll be right there, Guy. In just one minute. I promise."

The uniformed cops had gone back into the hallway to disperse the crowd of building tenants, including Carl and John, Ellen's next-apartment neighbors, who watched openmouthed as Taylor, his hand on a white velour shoulder, led Guy Adams out.

Kate shut the apartment door. Ellen made her way through the glass to the balcony. The curtain was a full billow in the gusty Santa Ana winds, and she pushed it aside, inspected her shattered door, the glass-strewn apartment. With a flick of her tennis shoe she broke off a wicked shard of glass protruding from the bottom of the door. She turned to Kate. "My hero," she said.

Kate, weak with laughter, finally had to sit down.

Ellen said, chuckling, "You have a wonderful laugh."

Kate gasped, wiping her eyes, "It feels terrific."

"As long as you've trashed my apartment," Ellen said, "Mother gave me this lamp. She visits here all the time. Would you mind?"

Kate inspected an orange lamp with a mushroom-shaped wicker shade. "It'll be a pleasure," she said, and hurled it to the floor.

"Thank you. Oh God, thank you. You were right about this apartment. It *is* easy to break into."

"I'll get this boarded up till it can be repaired." She wiped her eyes again. "Tell me what went on."

"He told me how it happened and why."

Kate said without a trace of regret, "We'll have a long night ahead, Ellen. We need a very detailed statement from you on tape and in writing. Everything you can remember, everything he—"

"Kate, I know it doesn't make sense to say that somebody could put a knife into somebody else's heart by accident, but that's really what he did."

"No malice? No intent?"

"No more than somebody stepping on a cockroach. What'll happen to him?"

"My guess is involuntary manslaughter. If adequate provocation can be proved. The test will be actual malice—or whether it was the sudden heat of passion. He may have to do a little time."

"Oh God, Kate. What will jail do to him?"

To soothe her, she said lightly, "He'll come through it all with class. Probably have a Persian rug in his cell."

Ellen smiled; Kate saw that she was drained. And it would be hours before they were through with the events of this night. She paraphrased Ellen's own invitation to her the night before: "I think it would be a good idea if you didn't stay here tonight." She added, "You have a friend who would like to put you up."

Ellen sighed. "I live with someone, as you very well know."

She looked at Kate and smiled. "And I've already misbehaved."

"Might as well be hung for a sheep as a lamb."

"In for a penny, in for a dime?"

"Six of one, half a dozen of another."

"That's enough, that's plenty, thank you."

Ellen went into the bedroom, soon reappeared with an overnight bag.

"Ellen," Kate said. "Before we go, before I have to get really busy on this case tonight—well, my situation...the way ... I—" She groped for words, not minding her awkwardness, only wanting the words to be the right ones. "I need time. But I could use ... a friend."

Ellen said slowly, "You're not the only one who needs time. I've learned a few things and I need to do some thinking, too... about a lot of things. I could use a friend, too."

Kate reached for her bag. "Let me take that."

"Not on your life, Detective Delafield. From now on I intend to handle what I can handle. You have a few things to learn about me."

"You'll take some getting used to."

Ellen said thoughtfully, "You know, my mother may just like you. She likes tough and capable people."

Kate said, grinning, "That's nice."

They left the apartment, Ellen's arm through Kate's. "I put a bottle of wine in my bag," Ellen said. "I'm sure we have something to celebrate."

Bella Books, Inc.

Women. Books. Even Better Together.

P.O. Box 10543
Tallahassee, FL 32302

Phone: 800-729-4992
www.bellabooks.com

Printed in the USA
CPSIA information can be obtained
at www.ICGtesting.com
JSHW021942030824
67469JS00001B/7